Abijah

and the American Revolution

Kenneth Wayne Virgil

Abijah and the American Revolution

Published by Wheatmark®
2030 East Speedway Boulevard, Suite 106
Tucson, Arizona 85719 USA
www.wheatmark.com

ISBN: 979-8-88747-267-6 (paperback)
ISBN: 979-8-88747-268-3 (ebook)
LCCN: 2025900378

Bulk ordering discounts are available through Wheatmark, Inc. For more information, email orders@wheatmark.com or call 1-888-934-0888.

Back cover photo of Abijah's headstone by P. Zucco.

To my family,
who never gave up on me

And for Smitty,
whose meticulous research
and commitment to our family's story
have provided us with an invaluable gift

Contents

Figures

Introduction

*I*n the heart of America's tumultuous journey to independence, there lived a man whose life bore witness to the birth of a nation. Abijah Virgil's story is one of humble beginnings in a rustic landscape, where the call of duty intersects with the ideals of liberty. As we embark on this narrative, we delve into a time when a fledgling nation's destiny hung in the balance, and the call to serve one's country echoed across untamed lands.

His life is a tribute to the steadfastness of those who toiled in the shadows of history, whose unwavering dedication shaped the very fabric of a nation. This story is about duty, sacrifice, and the steadfast spirit of a man who answered his country's call. He shaped his destiny and influenced the future of a young United States.

Abijah's story will resonate with many of us, not just as a historical account but as a reflection of our own experiences. It not only transports us to a time when life was simpler yet full of meaning and hard work, but it also allows us to connect with our ancestors and appreciate the generations before us who worked the land and preserved traditions. His dedication to daily chores and farming reflects a strong work ethic that many of us can relate to. In a world where hard work is often essential for survival, we understand the importance of toil and perseverance.

The central role of family and community in Abijah's life resonates with our understanding of the value of these bonds. The story emphasizes how families relied on each other and shared responsibilities to ensure everyone's well-being. His resourcefulness in using ashes as a natural fertilizer and making the most of every available resource is evidence of the people's ingenuity in a bygone era. It is a reminder of the importance of utilizing resources efficiently and sustainably—values that remain relevant today. Many of us yearn for a connection to nature and a simpler life in our fast-paced, modern world. The story also imparts valuable life lessons, such as patience, responsibility, and the importance of passing on knowledge through the generations.

Overall, Abijah's narrative allows us to step into a different time and place, reminding us of the timeless values and experiences that connect us across generations. It inspires us to appreciate the significance of hard work, family, and the land that sustains us.

On this journey through the awe-inspiring landscapes of Abijah's world, a time of uncertainty, sacrifice, and unyielding resolve, we unravel the chapters of his life, painting a vivid portrait of a man who lived through an era of revolution. His experiences uncover the untold stories that underpin America's exceptional emergence as an independent republic. I'll leave it to Abijah to impart the details in his own words . . .

1

Echoes of Time

*B*orn in 1758, I grew up on a farm near Green River, New York, one of the area's most rural and sparsely populated hamlets. As I tell my story, I hope you will find echoes of our shared humanity transcending time and place.

Let me take you back to the days of the American Revolutionary War, a time when everything felt uncertain and full of possibility. I grew up working on the farm, but my thoughts often wandered. Now and then, travelers passed through with stories about far-off places I couldn't picture. Hearing them made me restless, and I wondered what else might be beyond the fields. I couldn't help but dream about doing something different that mattered.

My name is Abijah Virgil. Though there is no official record of my birth date, my parents, William and Martha Virgin, always claimed I was born in

April 1758, so I have adopted this as my birth date. Due to the practical considerations of the time and the distance from the nearest church, I was baptized by Minister Gideon Bostwick of the Congregational Church in Great Barrington, Massachusetts, on November 1, 1759.

My parents chose my name carefully—Abijah, which comes from Hebrew and means "My Father is Yahweh." It wasn't a common name, but that's part of why they liked it; they wanted something unique that carried a sense of meaning. In the Bible, both Abijah, the king of Judah, and the son of the prophet Samuel were leaders in their time, though their lives weren't without flaws. My parents weren't looking for perfection—they saw the name as a reminder of strength, responsibility, and the potential to live a life guided by a higher purpose. For them, it wasn't about who these figures were in every detail but about the legacy of the name and the hope that I would carve out my path with integrity and determination.

I can see that my parents' last name and mine have confused you. Let me explain. By the end of the Revolutionary War, my brothers and sisters had changed their last name to Virgil, while our parents kept the original name. The surname Virgin has a long history in England with medieval roots as far back as the thirteenth century. However, it bears the shadow of our past support for the British Crown, especially during the French and Indian Wars of the mid-eighteenth century, when my grandfather fought for the Crown and its empire. But as times changed, so did our loyalties. Many from my generation supported the Patriots in the Revolutionary War, a shift that made us want to break away from the old ways and old names.

The name Virgil comes from the Roman poet Publius Vergilius Maro, who wrote about Aeneas, a wanderer and warrior who fled from Troy to carve out a new life across the sea, just as our family left England to carve out a new life in the colonies. Virgil was a student of Greek traditions such as Homer's *Iliad* and *Odyssey*. We made this choice to feel closer to the stories and ideas from ancient Greece and Rome. It really showed how we can adjust and grow.

Yet, Virgil was more than a nod to the classics. For us, it was an affirmation of the values we hold dear. Aeneas's journey was all about devotion to something bigger than himself, and that's how we saw our choice of Virgil. The name Virgil became both a link to a noble past and a beacon for the new world we sought to create.

My parents, William and Martha, were married in Ware River Parish, Hampshire County, Massachusetts in 1747. In November 1748, they welcomed their first child, James, born in Killingly, Windham County,

Connecticut. In 1753, two years after their marriage, they moved to Green River Hollow, near the hamlet of Green River, about eighty miles west of Ware River Parish. The rest of us, Asa, Bethiah, myself, and our other siblings, were born and raised there. My older siblings, especially James, Asa, and Bethiah, played a significant part in shaping my childhood under our parents' loving and nurturing care.

Green River is a small hamlet about six miles northeast of Nobletown. The hamlet is nestled in a narrow valley about three-tenths of a mile north of where the Green River and Cranse Creek meet. The area around us is hilly. To the southwest, there's Shepard Peak, which stands at about 1,625 feet, and to the northeast, there's Bald Mountain, rising to about 1,830 feet. The hills are generally rounded and great for growing crops, although some are steep. The soil is a mix of small rocks, sand, silt, and clay. It's known for being very fertile and suitable for growing plants because it drains well, holds moisture, and is rich in nutrients.

Because of the border arguments between the colony of Massachusetts (claiming all the land to the Hudson River) and New York (claiming large areas of what is now the county of Berkshire in Massachusetts), it was difficult for my parents to claim the land they lived on. Deemed as "squatters" or settlers without any legal right to the land they inhabited, they could not fulfill the requirements of either colony for land ownership. The transfer of legal ownership was only possible once the government had assigned the land.

But that did not mean they did not try. In 1757, my parents obtained a deed for their land by paying five and a half pounds to the Stockbridge Indians in Massachusetts. In return, they were given title to about two hundred acres of land. Stockbridge was established in 1734 and had strong ties with the Mohican Indians native to the Hudson and Housatonic River Valleys. In the 1700s, as the Mohican Nation faced increasing colonial pressures, they had to make a difficult decision. They decided to welcome an English missionary and resettle in a small portion of their ancestral lands, which gave rise to "Indiantown," or Stockbridge, as it is more commonly known.

Massachusetts said the deed was valid. However, New York did not share this recognition. The two finally settled the boundary when the Revolutionary War ended, and the land was placed in New York. This back-and-forth concerning land ownership is part of our family's complicated story. This problematic history of land and boundaries helps explain the story of our family's heritage.

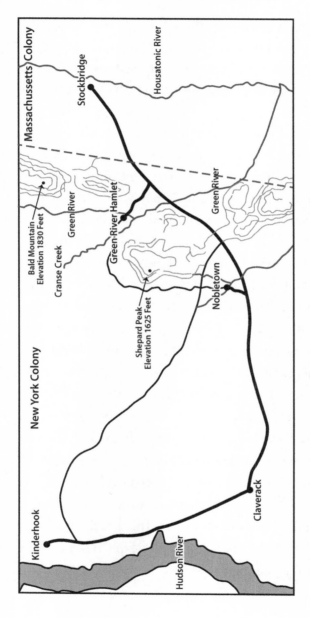

Figure 1 - Abijah's Hometown and Surrounding Area

Our family had expanded with two younger sisters, Mary, born in 1761, and Hulda, born in 1764. At the age of ten, I was becoming a lively farm boy. I took pride in my work on the farm and wanted to do my part. Each summer morning started the same, with the sun rising over the fields. I would head out to do my chores, knowing I was part of an ongoing effort of survival, carrying on the hard work and purpose my family had always lived by.

My story begins on a morning when our existence revolved around daily tasks that connected us to the land, livestock, and traditions passed down through generations. It was a world far from the complexities of urban life today. Yet, the desire for fulfillment and purpose remained timeless, bringing us closer to the land and connecting us across centuries.

As a child, my morning chores were to gather ashes from the fireplace and store them in the ash house, feed the chickens, gather their eggs, and milk the cows. Every morning before the fire could be re-kindled, I would take the ash shovel and scrape the gray and powdery remains from the hearth into a sturdy wooden bucket. I was cautious not to scoop up any hot embers because of the fire risk. The finer ashes, which felt soft like powder, were special. I'd put them in a bucket and carry them to our ash house, a small stone building just a short distance from the main house. Inside the ash house, we had barrels set up for different uses. The fine ashes went into the barrel marked "For Lye," which we used to make lye for soap. The coarser ashes, with little bits of wood still in them, had their place too. They went into another bin labeled "For Fertilizer." My father would take those ashes and spread them over our garden plot. They were important ingredients for helping the plants grow because they added nutrients to the soil.

Before continuing, let me explain our fireplace and how my mother made breakfast for us. We didn't have a stove, so everything was done over a large fireplace in our kitchen. It was a grand and vital part of our home. Once I had cleaned out the ashes and taken them to the ash house, Mother would start by rekindling the fire from the previous night's embers I had left. She would add a few pieces of wood, carefully coaxing the flames to life and slowly adding more wood to the fire for a steady, even burn.

The fireplace was big and sturdy, built from large, rough-hewn stones. It had a hearthstone, a flat, wide slab of stone, in front of the fire that was worn smooth from years of use. This hearthstone was more than just a place to stand. It was a work surface, a shelf, and sometimes even a seat when the weather was cold. My mother would set her pots and skillets on it, as it was large enough to hold several at once. The stone would warm up from the fire, keeping everything cozy.

A modest brick oven was nestled into the wall on one side of the fireplace. Shaped like a small dome, it resembled what some called a "beehive oven," about two or three feet wide and deep and just over a foot tall inside. Its sturdy iron door bore the marks of countless fires, while bricks blackened by years of soot and smoke lined its interior. My mother would build a fire inside, letting the flames heat the bricks. Once the bricks were hot enough, she swept out the ashes and slid the dough inside. The heat held in the bricks baked the bread perfectly every time. It was a simple setup, but it produced the most delightful bread that was crusty on the outside and soft on the inside.

The rest of the fireplace had an iron crane and hooks for hanging pots. The crane was a thick iron bar that could swing out over the hearthstone. My mother would hang a pot filled with water and oats for porridge, adjusting its position to control the cooking speed. Nearby, she'd have an iron skillet directly on the hearthstone for frying eggs or bacon. The crackling of the fire, the sizzle of the food, and the rich smells filling the room were all part of the morning ritual. Above the fireplace, herbs hung in neat bundles from the mantel, their earthy scents mingling with the cooking smells.

Several tools made the fireplace both functional and safe. A poker, or fire iron, was used to stoke the fire and adjust the logs, ensuring an even burn. Tongs allowed for the safe handling of hot logs and coals, while a shovel and broom made it easy to clean out ash and debris, keeping the hearth tidy and reducing smoke. Andirons, or fire dogs, supported logs to improve airflow, helping the fire burn hotter and more efficiently. Bellows were essential for directing air into the fire, reviving dying embers, or intensifying the flames. Finally, an ash bucket kept fuel or cooled ashes safely contained, making the fireplace a reliable source of warmth and light.

Imagine the firelight flickering on the stones and bricks while the smell of cooking fills the air. This was a space alive with care and activity, where our family came together not just to eat but to share time and leisure.

Now, back to my chores. After cleaning the fireplace, I would head to the chicken coop, let the chickens out, and throw some grain out to feed them. The hens would cluck and strut, their feathers ruffling as I approached. Then I would go into the coop, where the straw nests held their treasures of warm eggs, freshly laid, waiting for me to collect them. I could not help but laugh as I worked, the hens seemingly proud of their contribution to our daily lives.

I would return to the farmhouse carrying a basket filled with fresh eggs. Knowing how precious those eggs were, I was careful. Mother relied on them to prepare our morning breakfast, and I knew that even one broken egg could mean a missed meal.

After that, it was time to milk the cows. We had two milk cows, Bessie and Buttercup, and they were usually out grazing in the pasture that bordered the forest. To bring them in for milking, I would grab a bucket of grain from the feed room and walk to the pasture's edge, calling out, "Come, Boss, come, Boss." Bessie, the larger and older of the two, would always be the first to lift her head, her ears twitching at the sound of my voice. Buttercup, younger and more spirited, would often be the first to trot over, eager for the treat she knew I carried.

Once the cows came to me, I scattered some grain on the ground, allowing them to nibble, and gently looped a rope around their necks. Leading them back to the barn was easy, as both Bessie and Buttercup were familiar with the routine and trusted me.

Inside the barn, I would secure the cows in the wood-framed stanchions that held them in place while milking them. First, I would place a clean wooden bucket under Bessie's udder. Sitting on a low stool beside her, I would begin milking her. Milking the cows was a routine I quickly learned. I'd grip each teat firmly but gently, drawing out the milk in steady streams that hit the bucket with a satisfying rhythm.

Once I finished with Bessie, I would move on to Buttercup, repeating the process until both buckets were filled with frothy, warm milk. I would carry the heavy buckets back to the farmhouse. Inside, my mother would be waiting in the kitchen, ready to help with the next steps. We would separate the cream from the milk using the tried-and-true method my mother had learned from her mother. We poured the fresh milk into shallow pans and let it sit overnight in the cool pantry. By morning, the cream would have risen to the top.

Mother would skim the thick cream off with a spoon, careful not to waste a drop. The cream was set aside to be churned into butter, while the milk was used for drinking, cooking, and making cheese. I loved our rich, creamy butter, especially when I spread it thickly on warm bread fresh from the oven.

As I neared the farmhouse, the smell of breakfast cooking filled the air and made me smile. After a morning's work, the thought of a hearty meal was always welcome. Farm life had its meaning built on hard work, a bond with the land, and the family working together to keep things going.

After breakfast, as the warm rays of the morning sun fell on the earth, my father and I began our gardening routine. Helping my father plant and tend our family's crops was a valuable experience. As we worked the fields, he shared lessons about the different crops we planted. He taught me the careful art of planting and tending our crops. To him, corn, beans, and squash were more than just food—they were a part of our family's heritage. I learned to spread ashes to enrich the soil and keep pests away and about the importance of depth, spacing, and timing in everything we grew. Those moments gave me skills and values that stayed with me throughout my life.

Working in the fields taught me practical farming skills and the value of perseverance and patience. Farming requires a strong work ethic and careful attention to detail to bring life from the soil. Every task was a lesson in persistence, and I learned that with diligence and care, the land would reward you with abundance.

During the day, I helped my mother with household chores, learned to cook basic meals, and took care of my younger siblings. My older brothers would tell me about their experiences on the farm and teach me how to repair fences and use farm implements. These were my daily chores unless it was a Monday.

Mondays were washdays, which meant several trips to the well while Mother heated the water in large kettles. I would help my mother prepare the soap.

We used homemade soap crafted from lye and animal fat, a process I often helped perform. We would save animal fats, such as lard from pigs or tallow from cows and sheep. These fats were then put in kettles for heating. Then we would add the lye. We made our lye by leaching water through wood ashes. The strength of the lye solution could vary, which led to imprecision in soap-making. We would add water to dissolve the lye and mix it with the fats, stirring the mixture until it thickened and began to turn into soap. We then poured the mixture into molds to solidify, which we later cut into bars.

When the bars of soap were cut into small pieces and added to boiling water, a bubbly, soapy mixture was created. With the water hot and the soap ready, it was time to gather the laundry. Mother and my sister Bethiah sorted through the piles of clothes and linens, separating the whites from the colored fabrics. They carried the laundry to the washing area behind the barn, where a large wooden tub and washboard were set up.

We would start with the whites, soaking them in hot, soapy water and vigorously scrubbing each piece on the washboard, our hands working steadily. We worked through the pile together, occasionally adding hot water to keep the temperature right. After washing came the rinsing. I carried the heavy, wet clothes to the rinse tub filled with clean water, dunked each piece, and swished it around to rinse out the soap. Often, this step needed several rinses and extra trips to the well.

Wringing out the clothes was the next step. Bethiah and I would twist the garments tightly, squeezing as much water as possible out of them. The clothes were then draped over the long clothesline between two sturdy oak trees. Most days, the sun was high in the sky by that time, and a gentle breeze rustled the leaves, helping to dry the laundry throughout the afternoon.

Bethiah and Mother would prepare a starch solution for the linens as the clothes dried. They would mix a small handful of wheat flour into a bowl of cold water. The trick was to make it smooth, with no lumps, or it would ruin the clothes. The mixture was stirred with the back of a spoon until it looked like milk.

Then, they would heat water in a larger pot over the fire, bringing it to a simmer. Once the water was ready, they poured the flour mixture into the heated water slowly, stirring it to thicken evenly. It was ready when the mixture was clear enough to see the spoon. After letting the mixture cool, the linens would be dipped into the starch, wrung out, and then hung up to dry.

Once the clothes were dry in the late afternoon,

we removed them from the line. We folded each piece neatly and stacked them in a large wicker basket. Some of the items, like the linens, needed to be ironed. Mother and Bethiah heated the heavy iron over the fire, and together they pressed the linens, smoothing out the wrinkles and giving them a crisp finish.

The hot iron would set the starch, making collars stay stiff and skirts hold their pleats. It was a ritual for them, a moment to turn every day into something proper and presentable. I can still see Mother's hands, red from wringing out the cloth, and smell the faint warmth of the starch drying by the hearth. Whenever I press a shirt, I think of her standing by the fire, en-suring we all looked our best.

As the sun set, the day's work was finally done. The farmhouse was filled with the comforting smell of clean clothes and freshly baked bread, which Mother had prepared while the clothes dried. Wash day was hard work but brought a sense of togetherness and pride. I valued the time I spent with my mother and sister.

As the years went on, my work on the farm grew. I became essential to keeping our family fed and the farm running efficiently. The lessons I learned and the time I spent with my family in those fields stayed with me, shaping who I was and helping me carry on the farming way of life.

During the years before the American Revolution, my days were spent tending to the land and livestock. I couldn't help but notice the changes spreading through the colonies. My father would meet with neighbors on his trips to Nobletown and join their talk about their concerns over British rule. When he got home, the family would discuss what he had learned.

In December 1773, we heard about how some folks in Boston boarded a ship and threw its tea into the harbor. The news spread quickly and stirred up talk of defiance on our farm. My father and other farmers in the Hudson Valley expressed their support for the cause against British tyranny. We colonists did not like being taxed without representation in Parliament. As the British implemented additional taxes, the resentment from colonists like my father grew into anti-British sentiments.

The British responded to the events of the Boston Tea Party with punitive measures to reassert their authority and suppress the growing unrest and resistance within the American colonies. But their actions only stirred up more anger instead of calming things down. In Massachusetts and beyond, people saw these laws as unfair infringements on their rights like self-governance and fair trials.

The British thought their harsh rules would force

us to obey. They called them the Coercive Acts, but we called them the Intolerable Acts. Closing the port of Boston and taking away Massachusetts's rights were meant to punish and scare us. But instead of breaking us apart, it brought people closer together.

Around here, my father and his neighbors did not see it as just punishment; it felt like an attack on everyone's freedoms. We began to understand that if we did not stick together, we could lose the rights we had always believed belonged to us.

I didn't know much about what was going on, but I could feel something changing. My family didn't talk like they used to, and farming didn't seem like the only thing that mattered anymore. They looked worried, and I thought a significant event might be coming. War, they called it. I didn't know what it would mean for us, but I knew it would pull me away from the farm and into a new life I wasn't ready for.

2

The Militia

When I turned sixteen in April 1774, I was required to serve in the local militia. At that time, the American colonies had no professional army, so ordinary citizens like me and my family were called upon to defend our communities.

Before proceeding, let me provide some context about the military forces during the revolutionary struggle in the colonies. The Revolutionary War brought uncertainty and fear to every colony. People were wary of too much government control, so they turned to a different kind of military force called the militia. These militias initially formed as a practical necessity for local defense, as there was no standing army to protect the colonies from external threats, such as raids by Indigenous groups or attacks by rival European powers like the French or Spanish. Over time, the militias became a symbol of self-reliance and community unity, with neighbors banding together to safeguard their homes and towns.

As tensions with Britain escalated, colonial militias evolved from informal groups focused on local defense into a crucial force of organized resistance. The colonists' deep mistrust of standing armies, often viewed as tools of oppression, made militias the preferred means of safeguarding their liberties. British efforts to disarm these groups and suppress their activities only fueled the colonists' steadfastness, as they viewed the militias as a crucial expression of their right to self-governance and their duty to protect their communities and cherished ideals.

By the onset of the Revolution, militias had become more than a practical response to threats; they were a symbol of defiance against British authority. Their existence underscored the colonies' rejection of external domination and commitment to principles of freedom and self-governance. This blend of pragmatic defense, ideological conviction, and communal unity defined the role and significance of militias throughout the Revolutionary War.

In Green River, the local militia was a close-knit community affair. The town's men banded together in a company led by a steadfast captain or lieutenant. Ordinary farmers, blacksmiths, and shopkeepers were part of the militia, ready to defend their homes and families with the weapons and ammunition they each had on hand. Their commitment to duty depended on the threat level but was limited to three months and restricted to the borders of their colony. Every member had to attend to their livelihood, whether farming or storekeeping, besides serving in the militia. After their service ended, they could return to their everyday lives. Among these brave souls were the minutemen, an elite few who stood ready for a call to arms at a moment's notice. They were the first line of defense in times of peril.

Before I go on, I need to tell you a bit about the history of militias in New York. The first militia company in Albany County was formed in 1754, which was a big deal. It happened because of attacks by native groups from Canada on the town of Dutch Hoosick, up in northern New York. These raids spread fear into other areas, even reaching the quiet village of Stockbridge in Massachusetts. There, a man and his two children were killed by the same group, leaving the whole community shaken and grieving.

The raiders were likely natives from the Wabanaki Confederacy, an alliance of northeastern Indigenous nations that had been forced to relocate to Canada and aligned themselves with the French. The Wabanaki Confederacy had long resisted European settlers' encroachment and saw the alliance as a means to protect their homeland and sovereignty.

They were stirred up by the French, who were

aiming to halt British settlements right in their tracks. The French knew what they were doing, stirring up trouble to keep settlers like those in Dutch Hoosick from pressing deeper into areas that both France and Britain were contesting. This wasn't just a random raid. It was a more extensive strategy as the French and Indian War began. It was a way to intimidate settlers by conveying a stern message that these lands were not for the taking.

Realizing they needed a self-defense organization, the settlers in the area came together and organized their militia in Albany. Determined to protect their families, they required every able-bodied man between sixteen and sixty to join, a clear sign of their commitment to keeping their community safe.

Self-reliance and helping each other were a way of life in colonial America, and the militias showed just how serious folks were about protecting their homes and way of life without outside help. These militias in New York weren't just thrown together. They had a system to keep their settlements safe and to handle any threats that came their way. Each community took care of its militia, which was comprised of able-bodied men. They had their leaders, captains, lieutenants, and sometimes ensigns in charge, while the enlisted men made up the rest of the group and did most of the work.

Local militia officers had an important job when trouble came. They were the ones who sounded the alarm, figured out what was going on, and worked with nearby settlements to plan what to do next. They kept careful records, known as muster rolls, that listed the names of every member. When an incident occurred, messengers were sent out to gather the militia. Farmers who lived far from town got the message from riders on horseback so no one was left out. In bigger towns, the town crier would shout the news to rally everyone, while drums and horns were used to sound alarms and give signals when danger was near.

As things worsened between the colonies and Britain, a new kind of soldier appeared: the levies. Emerging during the Revolutionary War, levies were created to meet the need for a more mobile and long-serving force than the traditional militia. These men were picked from the militias and ordinary folks, answering a different call. Unlike the militia, they could be sent outside their colony and must serve for nine months. That meant leaving their homes and families, marching long distances, and fighting tough battles far away from everything they knew.

John Adams proposed the creation of a Continental Army to unify the militias under a centralized command, recognizing the need for a professional force to combat the British. During the chaos of the war, General George Washington implemented this vision, transforming the disorganized militias into a disciplined and effective fighting force. He believed a unified army was essential to challenge the British and unite the colonies under a common cause. These were no longer just farmers or townsfolk fighting temporarily—they became a professional army, trained and equipped to stand against the British and fight for independence. Their loyalty extended beyond their local colony; they were committed to the new United States they were striving to build.

The Continentals held the revolution together, enduring the harshest conditions as the war continued. And you know what? That's true. I lived through it myself. I've carried those memories ever since, heavy like the work we did back then. And those "harsh conditions"? They weren't just about the battles, not by a long shot. It wasn't just musket fire or bayonets tearing through men. The real fight was holding on to something human when it felt like our very humanity was being stripped away.

There were days, weeks even, where the cold was the only constant we knew. I remember my feet felt so numb I thought they'd gone to stone. We were never adequately clothed for the winter weather. At the Battle of Trenton, and I was there, our soldiers' thin coats, worn trousers, and improvised footwear were no match for the winter weather, leaving them vulnerable to frostbite. Many men wore worn-out boots or makeshift wraps around their feet, which offered little warmth or protection from the icy ground. Everything from uniforms to blankets became damp and froze in the cold, adding extra weight and discomfort to the already frigid conditions. I never got used to that cold, and even now, when winter comes, I feel in my bones a chill that won't leave.

Exhaustion was our constant companion. We'd march from dawn to dusk for days, sometimes through thick mud that pulled the boots right off our feet. Every muscle ached, and there wasn't time to rest. If we stopped, the British might push us back for good, so we kept moving. Some of us could hardly keep our eyes open, our minds numb from lack of sleep. I remember more than once falling into step in the dark of night, barely aware of where I was headed, just letting my legs carry me forward.

But maybe the most challenging ailment was the ache in my chest. Not the pain of muscle or bone, but the ache of knowing that I'd left my family, the farm, the place where I belonged. We were brothers-in-arms, bound by more than uniforms, but even that couldn't erase the emptiness. I carried their faces in my mind; the image of my mother's hands and the smell of home weighed on me as much as the musket slung across my shoulder. Those were the harshest conditions. They tried to break us in a thousand ways every day. But we stood firm and kept marching because, in the end, our fight was all we had left to hold onto.

But getting ready for war wasn't easy. Local governments didn't always have enough to go around, and there wasn't equipment for every militia member. So it fell to regular folks, farmers, and families to pitch in however they could. They gave what they had, even when they had little to spare. Each individual furnished their musket, blankets, powder horns, flints, and, on occasion, even a trusty tomahawk. In an era where the colonial governments could not consistently equip their militia members, the resourcefulness and ingenuity of the militias were admirable.

Even so, militias from different towns and counties had to work together when things got bad. When several companies joined, they made up regiments led by a colonel chosen by the local government. This kind of teamwork was crucial when they faced more significant threats. These collective efforts allowed for the pooling of resources and manpower, as well as the forming of alliances to protect more extensive regions, sometimes even entire colonies.

Muster days were a part of life for the militia. We'd gather to drill and be inspected, preparing ourselves for whatever might come. The training wasn't anything complicated, just the basic skills we needed to fight as a group. But those days weren't just about training; they brought us together and reminded us that we were all in this fight side by side. Each member was responsible for his weapons and gear, and every militiaman cherished his musket or rifle that symbolized his commitment to his community's defense.

Having turned sixteen, I was obliged to register at the nearest militia headquarters in Claverack, approximately ten miles west of our family farm near the Green River Hamlet. I made the journey to Claverack to register with the Albany County Militia, and I did so with pride.

Enlisting was a decision that thrust me into a world far removed from the familiar fields of my home. I was a young man, eager but inexperienced, embarking on a journey that would stretch the limits of my endurance and shape me into someone more than I had ever imagined.

Our militia unit convened one day a week in Claverack for several hours of training. Those training sessions were moments I eagerly anticipated. They made me feel like I was part of a cause of great importance.

Training days meant long hours of drills. Every drill was meant to turn us into a team that knew we could each count on one another. Going from the steady work of farm life to the strict demands of military training was a shock, but both were based on discipline. Every day pushed me harder than I thought I could handle, both in body and mind. The musket felt heavier with each passing hour, and the sergeants' commands seemed to go on forever.

Yet, within the hardships, I began to uncover a strength I hadn't known I possessed. The drills, though exhausting, were forging a new version of myself. I was learning the art of war—how to march in unison, handle a weapon with precision, and maintain a level of discipline that would be crucial in the heat of battle. Each day presented a new challenge, and I grew more resilient with each challenge.

The camaraderie within our ranks was a source of strength. We were a ragtag group of farmers bound together by a common cause. We shared our fears and frustrations, finding solace in each other's company. Our bond reflected the unspoken understanding that we were all navigating this unfamiliar path together.

Then, everything changed on that pivotal day of April 19, 1775.

3

Call to Arms

$\mathcal{W}$ednesday, April 19, 1775, was a day like any other.
I was out on the farm, tending to the usual chores.
The fields were gently glowing in the early morning
sun, and the air carried the crisp scent of spring. I was
completely unaware of what was happening about
150 miles east of the farm.

It was not until late the following day while in-
specting the crops that I heard a commotion. Couriers
on horseback were galloping throughout the countryside, urgently spreading the news from Lexington and
Concord. Their faces were determined and concerned,
and their message hung heavy. The first shots of the
American Revolution had been fired.

The news of British troops invading the countryside was sudden and shocking. It took us all by
surprise, creating a sense of fear and insecurity that

rapidly turned into anger. We felt that this aggression was a clear violation of our rights.

The announcement of the conflict at Lexington and Concord struck me deeply. My heart raced, and disbelief and anger washed over me. My father's stern face, usually stoic, now bore a mix of fear and determination. The peace of the farm felt like a completely different world compared to the ongoing battles happening elsewhere. Those couriers seemed like messengers from another world, bearing the weight of a revolution in their words. The anger was not just about the British attempting to take away arms and ammunition but also about their disregard for our rights as British subjects and their aggressive actions that threatened our way of life. It was a violation that we could not tolerate.

As I watched the couriers ride off to spread the news, it became clear that the life I had known was irreversibly altered. I realized that I, like so many others, had a role to play in this historic moment. The local militias were there to protect their rights and look out for their interests. When the British started shooting at them, everyone viewed it as a hostile and unwarranted act. It set off a chain reaction of resistance and rebellion across the land. The winds of revolution would sweep over the farm, my family, and the community I cherished. But we would not be divided. We would stand together, united, to defend our homes and fight for our freedom.

That's what I'd thought, but, in truth, we were more divided than I first believed. Sure, my family and the folks around us who shared our dreams of freedom were bound together, and our resolve hardened against the Crown. However, not everyone held the same fire in their hearts, not even in our communities.

Some colonists held beliefs that led them down a different path entirely, such as the Quakers or the Religious Society of Friends, who originated in England in the mid-seventeenth century and were committed to peace. They refused to take up arms regardless of the cause, as they believed all fighting was a betrayal of their faith and God's call to a life of peace. For this reason, the Quakers faced significant challenges and suspicion, as neither the supporters of the Crown nor the Patriots knew how to respond to their refusal to engage in the conflict. These peacekeepers often endured hostility and isolation, caught between the opposing forces of a war they could not support.

And it wasn't only the Quakers. The Moravians, Mennonites, and Dunkers, people I hardly knew until the war, stirred up talk of who was in and out, each with their unique history and beliefs. The Moravians, also known as the Unitas Fratrum (Unity of the Brethren), originated in the early fifteenth century in Bohemia and Moravia. The Mennonites emerged from the Anabaptist movement during the sixteenth-century Protestant Reformation, while the Dunkers, also called the Schwarzenau Brethren or German Baptists, began in Schwarzenau, Germany, in the early eighteenth century.

These people held firm in their beliefs, refusing to take up arms even as their neighbors braced for battle. We saw them in the fields, tending their work as usual, and some of us thought them cowards. But over time, I came to understand their kind of bravery. It takes courage to stand for peace in a world caught up in bloodshed. They faced suspicion, insults, and even threats, yet still, they held on to their faith.

So, while we thought of ourselves as one people and one colony, there was division even in our towns and fields. There were those of us ready to risk all for independence, others who clung to the security of Britain, and those who, in their way, risked just as much to keep from spilling blood at all. Perhaps we weren't all united in purpose, but in those years, I learned that conviction comes in many forms. And in our ways, we each found courage to face the uncertain days ahead.

Word came that colonists from various regions rallied to support Massachusetts and to prepare for the possibility of further military actions by the British.

In a few days, about sixteen thousand men marched in small bands upon Boston to protest and resist further incursions. Fights broke out between Crown supporters and rebels as the insurrection spread through the areas surrounding Boston, and groups of rebels harassed the redcoats wherever they appeared.

It wasn't as simple as one side against the other; not all colonists saw rebellion as the right course. Those loyal to the Crown, known formally as Loyalists, weren't all wealthy merchants or king's men, though many merchants feared that independence would sever their ties to British trade. Patriots, however, often derided them as Tories, a term meant to vilify their allegiance and paint them as enemies of liberty. For some, loyalty was less about wealth or politics and more about a deep kinship with Britain. Stories and songs from generations are still rooted in the old country. Others believed that a British government, broken as it was, held more order than any new government we could build from scratch. They feared the chaos rebellion might bring, war tearing apart their lives and families. Some, out of deep religious belief, thought it was wrong to rise against the king, seeing rebellion as a step away from God's order.

Soon, the British found themselves confined to Boston and the surrounding area. With our camps surrounding the city, those Loyalists now saw the full weight of war descending upon them. Some held out for Britain with the same strength of mind as we held out for freedom, each side bracing for a protracted confrontation.

I waited to see if the Albany County Militia would be called to arms. The county did not respond as a militia unit, staying in New York. Still, it was not for lack of will but a combination of geographic distance, the imperative of local defense, limited resources, coordination challenges, and differing regional priorities that led to their non-participation in these early incidents. Their focus remained on protecting their communities and responding to the needs of their region during those critical times in American history.

My decision was clear. I gathered my equipment, bade farewell to my family, and set off toward the east, toward Boston. The journey would take time, and there was no doubt it would be uncertain. But I was not alone. I crossed paths with others who felt the same burning drive. Together, we joined Captain Joseph Thompson's company, a part of the 6th Massachusetts Regiment led by Colonel John Nixon, rushing toward Boston, where history unfolded and where my life, like countless others, would be forever changed. It was a journey of personal sacrifice and commitment, authenticating the bravery of the American people.

4

The Siege of Boston

*B*ritish troops had arrived in Boston in October 1768, several years before the outbreak of fighting at Lexington and Concord. These soldiers were no ordinary men. They were the professional backbone of the British army—trained, disciplined, and equipped to maintain British authority and enforce the laws of the Crown. At that time, Boston was still under a civilian government, and the local authorities held the reins of power.

However, even in those early days, tensions between the American colonists and these well-drilled British troops had been simmering for years. We could feel the storm brewing on the horizon. It all came to a head in 1773 when the British Parliament decided to impose a tax on tea, known as the Tea Act. The tax and other grievances made colonists feel unfairly taxed without a say in the decisions made so far away. During the Boston Tea Party, members of the Sons of Liberty, a patriot resistance group, led the protest against taxation without representation by dumping 340 chests of British East India Company tea into Boston Harbor on December 16, 1773. Disguised as Mohawk Indians to conceal their identities, they carried out the act as a bold statement against British control over colonial trade. Though it was initially called the "destruction of the tea," newspapers and later accounts popularized the name "Boston Tea Party" as a symbol of defiance.

In 1773, the cost of tea became both a financial and symbolic factor in the growing anxieties between the colonies and Britain. A single chest of tea at the time typically held around 350 pounds and was valued at approximately £10 to £20, depending on the type. This was a significant amount of money, equivalent to more than a year's earnings for many laborers.

The Boston Tea Party caused the British East India Company to lose over £9,600, an enormous financial blow. In modern terms, this amount would equate to over $1.7 million, highlighting the event's magnitude as a protest and an economic disruption.

However, the cost of the tea went far beyond its monetary value. The destruction of the tea was a direct challenge to British authority and taxation policies, particularly the Tea Act, which colonists viewed as a violation of their rights. This act of defiance led to severe repercussions, including the Coercive Acts, further inflaming hostilities and setting the colonies toward revolution.

The price of tea, then, was not just measured in pounds or dollars but in its role as a catalyst for war. It symbolized the colonists' refusal to accept what they saw as unjust control and taxation, marking a turning point that led to years of struggle and, ultimately, independence.

After the Boston Tea Party, the British enacted strict measures to discipline the colonists for their defiance. The measures taken only heightened the dissatisfaction of the already disgruntled American colonists.

Many colonists began to sense that a conflict with the British authorities was becoming increasingly likely during the early 1770s. Anticipating these brewing apprehensions, colonial militias and local governments started stockpiling ammunition and weapons like the ones in Lexington and Concord. The goal was to be ready for whatever might come our way. We understood the importance of safeguarding our communities against potential threats, whether they were hostile Native American forces or, as it turned out, British troops.

The British government, on the other hand, viewed our preparedness with suspicion and concern. They believed that the stored munitions were intended for use against British forces. This fear of our growing resistance led the British authorities to attempt to confiscate the colonial munitions. This, in turn, set off the Battles of Lexington and Concord on that fateful day of April 19, 1775, when shots echoed through the Massachusetts countryside.

Soon after those initial battles, British authorities began replacing civilian officials with military officers. The British military took over, declaring martial law and imposing curfews. The city that had once been under civilian government now began to see the military's influence take hold. Our beloved Boston was caught in the grip of change, with the April 19, 1775, events setting the wheels in motion for the tumultuous times ahead.

By June 1775, Boston was under British control, and the American forces had essentially laid siege to the city. The Sons of Liberty members learned that the British intended to move troops to the high-ground positions of Breeds Hill and Bunker Hill on Charlestown Neck. These positions were strategically vital as they overlooked Boston and its harbor. Controlling these hills would allow the British to dominate the area with artillery and expand their hold on the city. Recognizing the urgency, Major General Israel Putnam and the Massachusetts Committee of

Safety took swift action, ordering Colonel William Prescott and his regiment to fortify Breed's Hill and Bunker Hill on June 16, 1775, securing the strategic high ground before the British could establish their position. Prescott's regiment began constructing defensive positions across the Charlestown Peninsula and Breed's Hill during the night.

While our regiment did not arrive in time to help build the redoubts and entrenchments, we were among the first to rush to Charlestown Neck and Breed's Hill to fortify the American position.

Breed's Hill offered an ideal vantage point to oversee Boston and its harbor. It allowed our forces to closely monitor the British movements and control access to the city. We knew that if we could secure the hill, it would disrupt the British supply and reinforcement routes by sea.

However, there was more to it than just strategy. Symbolism played a significant role in our decision to hold that ground. The British believed they were invincible. But they underestimated our resolve and capabilities. Therefore, defending Breed's Hill was not just a military move. It was a statement to show that we, the colonists, were ready to stand up and protect our rights and liberty.

Prescott was in charge of building a redoubt. A

redoubt is like a makeshift fort with a raised earthen wall about six feet high with ditches in front of it. Those ditches were crucial, making it much harder for the British to overrun us. They had to climb down and then climb up that wall to take the position.

That was not all. Prescott's men built breastworks, low barriers made of earth and logs, in front and on the sides of the redoubt. These breastworks provided us with extra cover and protection. In addition, the men dug trenches, creating defensive positions where our soldiers could shelter from enemy fire while still aiming at the approaching British troops.

Then there were abatis. These were barricades they set up with felled trees, their sharpened branches and stakes pointing outward, making them formidable obstacles for the enemy. They placed multiple abatis before the breastworks and redoubt to slow the British advance. By taking these defensive measures, the men aimed to maximize the effectiveness of their limited forces. We needed to conserve our ammunition and make every shot count.

On the morning of June 17, my unit and I took positions in the breastworks just east of the redoubt. These defenses extended in a V-shaped line of entrenchments, providing some cover against the British advance. Alongside Colonel Brewer's regiment from Massachusetts, we held the ground at a hay breastwork that extended from the redoubt and followed the rail fence. Below the hill, the rail fence, reinforced with hay, sloped downward toward a small bluff by the water's edge, where makeshift barricades of stones and fencing lined the shoreline.

To our left were Colonel Ephraim Doolittle's and Colonel Ebenezer Woodbridge's regiments. Both regiments were from Massachusetts. East of them, down to the edge of the water, were Colonel James Reed's and Colonel John Stark's regiments from New Hampshire.

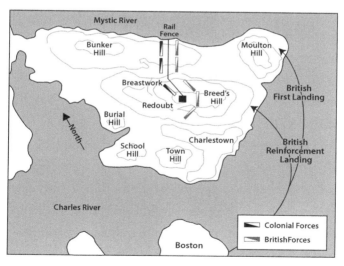

Figure 2 - Bunker Hill: Battle Positions and Unit Movements

After we arrived, the British forces began their advance toward Charlestown. The sight was formidable and impressive, showcasing their military prowess and the gravity of the impending conflict. Over 2,200 redcoats were ferried across the Charles River in flat-bottomed boats known as bateaux. These boats were selected for their ability to quickly land on the Charlestown Peninsula, directly accessible from Boston. The shallow waters and tidal conditions in the area drove this choice.

The British formed, their uniforms bright in the sun for a two-prong attack. Half approached the Mystic River, engaging companies from the regiments of Doolittle, Woodbridge, Reed, and Stark. Those American companies organized themselves into three ranks and maintained a withering fire on the British. It was incredible. The British line crumbled as they took hit after hit. They had to retreat.

Then, just moments later, the other half of the British force started advancing on our position. The hill was steep, and the top of it stood over sixty feet above sea level. The grass was tall and thick, challenging for the British soldiers to march across, and they had to step over stone walls as they climbed. It was a harrowing sight, seeing those British soldiers so close as we held our fire, the pressure mounting with each passing second.

As I stood on the battlefield at Breed's Hill, the air was thick with smoke from the British warships cannonading our positions, and the sound of explosions was deafening. I was scared, and I gripped my musket tightly, heart pounding in my chest, as the British soldiers advanced in their first assault on the hill. Their red coats were starkly contrasted against the dusty ground, and the unease in the air was unmistakable.

I remember clearly what Prescott told us. He stood firm, looking out at the advancing British troops, then turned to us with a calm but commanding voice. "Boys," he said, "hold your fire. Don't shoot until you see the whites of their eyes." He wanted to make sure we didn't waste a single shot, only firing when we were sure to hit our target. It was crucial because we only had twelve to fifteen cartridges each, and every shot had to count. His words stayed with me, a reminder of the discipline and resolve we needed in that desperate moment.

We fired our volleys when the order was given, and all hell broke loose. The noise, the shouts, the chaos, it was overwhelming. Amidst it all, I suddenly felt a sharp, searing pain in my leg. I stumbled, almost falling, and looked down to see a musket ball had struck me just above the knee. Blood began to soak through my breeches, and my leg throbbed with pain.

Despite the wound, I knew I couldn't stop. The adrenaline was pumping through me, keeping me upright. I gritted my teeth and continued to load and fire my musket, determined to hold our position. The smoke was so thick it was hard to see the enemy, but we knew they were pushing forward tenaciously.

As that first assault finally faltered and the British began to fall back, I stood there, breathing heavily. I glanced down at my leg again; the wound wasn't fatal, but it was bad enough. I knew I had to be ready for the next wave, even though the pain was becoming more severe. I sat down on the ground and used water from my canteen to wipe the blood away so I could see the damage. Fortunately, the ball hit me at an angle and went clean through the leg, not hitting the bone. I continued to clean and bandage the wound, stopping the blood loss. Looking around me, I realized how fortunate I was as I saw the dead and seriously wounded being carried off the hill. Little did I know, this was only the beginning of the day's challenges, and I would soon face more than I could have imagined.

After pushing them back the first time, we knew they were coming again. From our position, we could see them reorganizing at the base of the hill. The officers shouted orders, and the soldiers reloaded and prepared for another charge. Despite the chaos, they were disciplined and determined.

When they started up the hill again, the air was thick with smoke and the roar of cannon fire. We held our fire, waiting for them to get closer, just as Prescott had instructed. The tension rose again. As they advanced, we could see their faces, set with determination and anger.

Then, all at once, we opened fire. The noise was deafening, and the air filled with the acrid smell of gunpowder. I felt a sharp sting in my shoulder during the thick of the fight. I realized I'd been hit, but the wound wasn't deep. The pain was manageable, and a comrade quickly wrapped a bandage around it to stem the bleeding. I had no time to dwell on it; the fight was too critical, and we couldn't afford to lose ground. So I picked up my musket and fought against the advancing redcoats.

The enemy was getting closer, and the noise was deafening. It felt like the whole world was collapsing around us. Just as I steadied myself for another shot, I felt a searing pain in my side. It was like a hot iron had been driven into me. A musket ball had pierced me, and the pain was so intense that I couldn't hold onto my weapon. It clattered on the ground as I fell, the world spinning around me.

I hit the ground hard, gasping for breath. The battle raged on around me, and I could hear the shouts of my comrades and the cries of the wounded. The pain was overwhelming, and I could feel myself slipping in and out of consciousness. There was no time for anyone to check on me. Everyone was fighting desperately to hold the line.

The world seemed distant as I lay there. The sounds of the battle faded in and out, and everything felt surreal. I tried to stay awake and focus, but it was hard. The pain in my side was increasing, and my vision blurred. All I could do was hope that my comrades could hold their ground and that the sacrifice we were all making would not be in vain.

It was a moment of sheer madness and desperation. The battle raged savagely, and the stakes were high. We were fighting for our freedom and our future. Unable to move and the pain nearly unbearable, I knew that I had given everything I could.

When the British finally retreated, a small party of men came to check on the wounded. They saw I was still alive and carried me off the field to a surgeon. I was not the only one wounded. Colonel Nixon himself was severely injured in the thigh. We were all paying a heavy price for our stand that day.

Having been carried back to a field hospital in the rear area, I was not there when the British took the redoubt. The British had received reinforcements of about six hundred men between the second and third attacks. The Americans still there fired a couple of volleys, and, out of ammunition, the fight turned into hand-to-hand combat. Despite heavy casualties, they held the line as long as possible, but the British forces ultimately overwhelmed our positions. Despite their losses, Nixon's regiment was among the last to retreat as our troops fell back, allowing the British to secure the high ground. It was a costly victory for them, with many lives lost. The battle may have changed the immediate landscape but did not break our spirit.

This battle was my stark introduction to the violence and intensity of warfare. I felt fear, yes, but also a stubborn will to stand my ground. Each volley of musket fire, each command barked by the officers, each fallen comrade—these were the harsh realities I faced. Yet, in the heat of battle, I found a strange clarity. My resolve hardened, and the sense of purpose I had felt when enlisting became more profound.

Released from duty in August 1775, I returned home to rest and recuperate. My family was excited to see me, and their warm welcome was a balm to my weary spirit. I used the time to regain my strength, though I did help with some of the easier chores around the farm. The familiar sights of Green River seemed almost foreign now, as though I had changed more profoundly than I had imagined. My older brothers, James and Asa, were still serving with the Albany County militia, but my sister Bethia, who had married in 1771, now had two young children. To my surprise, my parents had welcomed a new son into the family, my youngest brother, Jacob. The war had etched its mark on me; I was no longer the boy who had left for battle. I had faced death, learned toughness, and discovered a new sense of purpose.

When the call to arms resounded, it stirred a deep sense of duty within me, igniting a steely perseverance and commitment to defend my country. This was the beginning of a journey that would test my courage and fortitude, and the lessons learned in those early days would become my guiding light through the trials and triumphs that lay ahead.

By December 7, 1775, I had recovered enough to enlist in Captain Thompson's company for one year, joining the regiment stationed at Winter Hill in Somerville, Massachusetts. We were known as the 6th Massachusetts Regiment then, but not for long. A few weeks later, on January 1, 1776, we were consolidated and redesignated as the 4th Continental Regiment. That meant our regiment merged with another, combining what was left of two Massachusetts units into a single body. The army was tightening its ranks, replacing the patchwork of state militias with a unified structure under General Washington's command. It wasn't just about changing our name. It was about making us part of a larger entity, a continental army that stood together as one force, no matter where we hailed from. It felt like stepping into something more significant than the fight in Massachusetts. It was about the whole country now.

Upon rejoining my fellow soldiers, I found Boston embroiled in a precarious American siege. Leading our army, General Washington had expertly blockaded the British forces, trapping them without land access and forcing them to rely solely on risky supply and reinforcement routes across the sea.

The streets of Boston echoed with the sounds of a different kind of war now, one marked by sporadic raids, fleeting skirmishes, and the silent menace of sharpshooters concealed in the shadows. The biting grip of winter had taken hold, and firewood had become a treasure so scarce that we, in our desperation, resorted to felling trees and dismantling wooden structures.

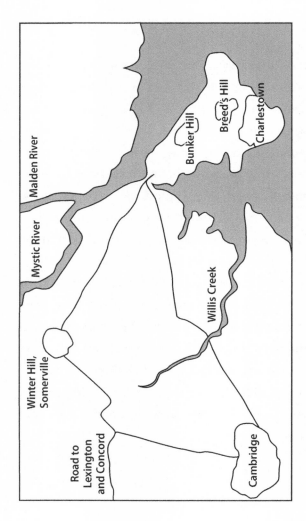

Figure 3 - Winter Hill Encampment, Somerville, Massachusetts

The city's hardships multiplied as brutal winter storms swept in, and the rise of American privateers added to the British plight. A makeshift American war fleet, consisting of a dozen converted merchant ships, had taken to the seas and captured over fifty British vessels during the frigid months. Many of these seized ships were laden with vital sustenance for the British troops. Hunger gnawed at the very core of the British ranks, and whispers of desertion filled the air. Scurvy and smallpox had also reared their dreadful heads within the city's walls.

Yet, as we kept our watch, General Washington's army grappled with its peculiar woes. Gunpowder had become as rare as a sliver of sunshine in those grim days. Some of our comrades had to wield spears instead of muskets, a sight that spoke volumes of our struggles. Many of us toiled without pay, and the expiration of numerous enlistments loomed at year's end.

Smallpox, an insidious adversary, threatened both sides. Inoculation, a method known as variolation, was used to shield against the pox. It involved a careful incision and the introduction of live virus-laden threads into the flesh. Some believed this procedure was more dangerous than facing the disease itself, despite evidence to the contrary. The clergy, invoking God's wrath, decried inoculation, arguing it interfered with divine will.

General Washington was a wise and cautious leader and opted for a strict quarantine, isolating those afflicted with the pox, be they soldiers or civilians. Townsfolk showing symptoms were confined to the hamlet of Brookline, while afflicted soldiers found their way to a quarantine hospital nestled by a quiet pond near Cambridge.

Such was the grim picture, with American and British forces at a stalemate, a chess game where neither side would yield. It was a contest of wills, a battle of endurance, until one day in March of 1776, when General Washington put artillery on Dorchester Heights. The artillery had a commanding view of Boston and the harbor, and their use made the city and ships in the harbor vulnerable to attack and destruction. General William Howe's position was unsustainable. As the British Commander-in-chief, he decided it was time to break the deadlock and abandon the beleaguered city of Boston, taking his forces northward to Halifax in Nova Scotia.

5

Dark Days

*F*ar from over, the war was beginning to develop, and our military leaders prepared for years of combat. There was no turning back. While the British were evacuating Boston, it became clear that New York City would be their next target. Washington ordered us to New York, and on April 1, 1776, we left Somerville, Massachusetts, and began marching about ninety miles to New London, Connecticut, at the mouth of the Thames River. We could only advance fifteen to twenty miles daily. The typical spring weather, cold and wet with the frost just leaving the ground, sometimes made the dirt roads a muddy quagmire. We reached New London on the ninth of April.

We set sail for New York on April 11, 1776, in what I can only describe as a fool's gamble with the weather. A blinding snowstorm swept through that morning, making it hard to see your hand in front of your face. Still, the order was given, and we boarded the ships with snow piling on our hats and shoulders. It was very cold, and the wind tore at the sails as we pushed off into Long Island Sound.

The storm made everything ten times harder. The strong wind didn't seem to know what direction it wanted to go, tossing us one way and then another. The snow soaked through our clothes and turned to icy slush beneath our boots. Visibility was near zero, and even the most experienced sailors among us looked uneasy, squinting through the whiteout as if they could clear the storm.

Once the storm passed, the trip didn't get much more manageable. The wind was fickle, often working against us, and when it died down entirely, we sat motionless, the ships bobbing in the water like corks. The cold rain came next, relentless and chilling us to the bone. When we reached Hell Gate, we had to wait for the tides to shift before daring to pass through its treacherous waters. Some of us joked that the gate was named for the misery we'd endured the whole trip.

And then there was the ever-present threat of British patrols. Even with the weather on our side as cover, we kept a sharp eye on the horizon, knowing that an encounter with the enemy could turn this miserable journey into a disaster.

By the time we finally arrived in New York City

on April 17, we were thoroughly beaten down by the journey. Snow, rain, tides, and cold seemed like nature had thrown everything at us to keep us from reaching our destination. But we made it. We stumbled off those ships wet, freezing, and exhausted but ready to press on. If nothing else, that miserable trip reminded us of the endurance this war would demand, not just on the battlefield but every step or sail along the way.

New York City emerged as a pivotal player in the 1776 American Revolutionary War. Following their expulsion from Boston, the British set their sights on New York City, recognizing its potential to serve as a stronghold and a launchpad for their colonial operations. Positioned strategically on the northeastern coast of North America, New York City held the key to controlling crucial maritime routes, particularly the entrance to the Hudson River.

The Hudson River was more than just a waterway. It was the lifeline of transportation and communication, connecting the Atlantic Ocean to the interior of North America. It was a watershed moment, and the British knew that. Control of New York allowed them to dominate this essential waterway, influencing trade and troop movements.

New York was ideal for the British to set up a base. British forces were primarily concentrated in Canada during the early stages of the war. They needed a secure supply route to the American colonies, and the Hudson River was the perfect solution. It was like an artery connecting them to Canada.

Moreover, New York City's harbor was a naval base to envy. It was one of the best natural harbors on the east coast of North America, providing a safe anchorage for British naval vessels and allowing them to project power along the coast and engage with the American Continental Navy.

Now, let me tell you about Governors Island. This island sat right at the entrance to New York Harbor on the southern tip of Manhattan Island, and controlling it was vital. It was about seventy acres in size, and whoever held it had control over access to the city's harbor. This strategic location allowed for the interception of enemy ships and the city's protection from naval attacks. When General Washington arrived in New York in April 1776, he knew he had to defend this key location.

Upon our arrival on April 17, Washington immediately dispatched us to Governors Island. Our unit's role was crucial. We toiled tirelessly, digging ditches to impede any potential landing force and using the excavated dirt and rocks to erect stone walls and bastions. These bastions, equipped with gun platforms for artillery, sally ports for secure entry and exit, and parapets to minimize our exposure to enemy fire, reflected our dedication and the importance of our mission.

We included furnaces next to the gun platforms to fire heated shots, an ammunition type used against ships. We would heat the cannonballs until red-hot and then quickly load them into the cannons. When fired, the red-hot shot could ignite anything flammable on an enemy ship, thus potentially causing fires.

And here's the thing—British ships of the time were constructed with wooden hulls and superstructures and had all sorts of flammable materials, from tar and pitch to rigging and sails. They were like floating tinderboxes. So, if a heated shot landed on one of those ships, it could spell disaster. Their wooden construction, openings like gun ports, and storage of gunpowder and provisions below deck made them susceptible to catastrophic explosions and fires.

We also built secure storehouses for ammunition, food, and supplies. These were sheltered by thick stone walls and protected by several feet of dirt. Of course, we also needed infrastructure for the soldiers like barracks and storage facilities.

We spent the summer working day and night, and by August 1, having completed all that construction, we were ready to defend the harbor. It was a pivotal moment, and we were prepared to play a vital role in protecting New York during those challenging times.

Figure 4 - Hudson River Entrance and the Strategic Importance of Governors Island

The summer of 1776 was a time of foreboding for the American cause. General Washington was still figuring out the British strategy and where they would launch their attack. Both Manhattan Island and Long Island were strategically essential locations. By positioning troops on both islands, he aimed to cover both possibilities. Meanwhile, the British juggernaut began its steady landing of troops on Staten Island at Watering Place on July 2, and as the weeks passed, their numbers swelled to a massive force that loomed ominously in our thoughts.

On August 27, it became apparent that the enemy's focus was Long Island as the British launched their attack, landing approximately fifteen thousand troops at Gravesend Bay. The Battle of Long Island was a grueling contest, a day when the rumble of artillery and the crackle of musket fire painted a bleak picture. Yet, our troops fought with unwavering grit and tenacity. However, the British outflanked them in a brilliant tactical maneuver, forcing a retreat across the East River to Manhattan Island at Brooklyn Ferry. The defeat at Long Island was a harsh blow to endure. What followed were the dark days that tested the very mettle of our young nation. Ultimately, we were thrown out of New York and chased across New Jersey and into Pennsylvania, our spirits battered and our hopes dwindling.

Between August 29 and 30, we evacuated our troops from Governors Island and Long Island. It was a harrowing retreat, with the British fleet firing on us. We managed to escape as the British forced us out of New York City, which would remain under British control until the end of the revolution in 1783. Having ceded Governors Island, our regiment fell under Major General Joseph Spencer's command. On a bustling September 1, we made our way to Manhattan Island, tasked with manning three lines of entrenchments, like the threads of a web, along Harlem Heights, just eight miles north of the vibrant heart of New York City.

Our stay on Manhattan Island was not one of idle days. Several engagements marked it, each etched into my memory like the pages of a tale. September 16 stands out as our single moment of triumph that summer. It was there, at Harlem Heights, that we managed to push the British back and force them to retreat. It was a small battle, but it demonstrated our soldiers' bravery, a source of pride for our young nation.

Yet, with his crafty tactics, British officer Howe did not let defeat deter him. He set sail with a formidable force, navigating the treacherous East River waters past Hell Gate. His destination was Throggs Neck, a tiny island separated from the mainland by a meandering creek and unforgiving marshes.

Prescott's regiment had already dug in at the creek's edge, stubborn as ever. Washington dispatched our unit and Brigadier General James Varnum's Rhode Islanders to reinforce Prescott's steadfast band. Now totaling 1,800 men, the American forces formed an unyielding barrier that Howe's forces could not breach. The British stood at a standstill despite several attempts, trapped in a defensive posture for six long days.

Then, as autumn leaves whispered secrets to the wind, General Howe had his army set sail from the shores of Throggs Neck Island. With their sights set on Pell's Point, they began their advance toward White Plains on October 16. Meanwhile, my unit had been given new orders and were beckoned farther north to North Castle, where we laid the groundwork for our defensive positions.

On October 28, we received the sad news that Washington had been defeated in a heated battle at White Plains. For the following days, General Howe, in a calculated move, strengthened his position and waited for further reinforcements. With a heavy heart, Washington organized his weary army for a tactical retreat into the sheltering embrace of the hills.

As the ghosts of October's past haunted us on the night of the thirty-first, Howe devised his strategy for the morrow while Washington, mindful of his men, began the slow retreat northward to North Castle. Surprisingly, General Howe chose not to follow, instead turning his gaze southward, seeking to rid Manhattan Island of the Continental Army presence by taking Fort Washington.

Washington, in response, led his army farther

north to Peekskill and crossed the Hudson into New Jersey. General Nixon divided his forces at Peekskill, sending those fit for battle to join Washington's ranks while the sick and wounded remained behind, nursing their ailments in the quaint town.

November's bitter chill bore down upon us as our unit, in the company of General Washington's army, embarked on a southward journey across the Hudson River toward Fort Lee. The November rains and frigid nights only compounded our misery. The pressure from the British had left us in dire straits. We found ourselves without the shelter of tents, scarcely possessing a handful of blankets, our garments hanging in tatters. Many of us lacked shoes or stockings. For some, only linen drawers and a hunting shirt offered modest protection from the elements.

British officer General Charles Cornwallis's obsessive pursuit prompted our urgent departure from New Jersey. Following the capture of Fort Washington by Howe's forces, Cornwallis relentlessly crossed the Hudson River and swiftly advanced upon Fort Lee, affording us minimal time to make our escape. With little more than the clothes on our backs, we managed to flee Fort Lee with what supplies we could gather as we made our way to safety. The soldiers' perseverance during this problematic retreat reflects their strength in adversity.

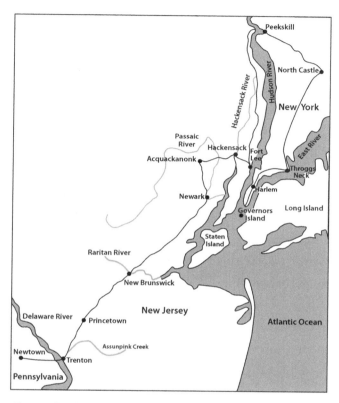

Figure 5 - Escape and Movement: Abijah's Route from Governors Island to Newtown

On November 21, we crossed the Hackensack River into Hackensack, New Jersey, and continued to Acquackanonk, crossing the Passaic River. After crossing the bridge over the Passaic River, we swiftly burned it to impede Cornwallis's pursuit as we moved into Newark. Departing Newark on the twenty-eighth, our timing was critical, for as our rear guard left from the south, Cornwallis's forces entered from the north, intensifying our predicament.

On December 1, approximately two thousand of Washington's depleted and weary men, grappling with setbacks, seemingly never-ending marches, hunger, and dwindling supplies, decided to depart. This marked a disheartening chapter in our campaign. Major General William Stirling's men, who had previously served as our army's vanguard, now became our rear guard as we made our way to New Brunswick. On December 2, Washington led the army to Princetown; by December 3, we had reached Trenton. There, we gathered all available boats both north and south of Trenton along the Delaware River, and we either used them for crossing into Pennsylvania or burned them to prevent the British from utilizing them.

General Cornwallis had our rear guard, the men under Stirling's command, in his sights on December 2, but orders from General Howe mandated that he maintain his position until Howe arrived. It was not until December 6 that Howe's forces finally converged with Cornwallis's. This four-day delay proved our saving grace, allowing us to cross the Delaware at Trenton and eventually find our way to Newtown in Pennsylvania. As the last of our men barely crossed into Pennsylvania, Cornwallis's troops entered Trenton, frantically scouring the area for boats to pursue us, but their efforts proved vain. All the boats had been set ablaze or transported to Pennsylvania with Washington.

General Howe, fully aware of the pitiful state of the ragtag forces remaining under Washington's command, coupled with the impending end of most, if not all, of our troops' enlistments within the next three weeks, decided to abandon the chase. He dispersed his troops to various posts in New Jersey, such as Pennington, New Brunswick, Trenton, Bordentown, and Princetown. From these positions, he could keep an eye on the smoldering rebellion, gather intelligence, and plan to renew his campaign in the spring when he intended to end what he viewed as a regrettable and distasteful affair.

My enlistment was nearing expiration, and the morale in our camp was at an all-time low. The British had driven us out of New York City, and Congress had abandoned Philadelphia, our nation's capital, due to the looming threat of a British attack. As Congress relocated to Baltimore, it felt like the cause for independence was slipping through our fingers, and many of my fellow soldiers had deserted. These were indeed dark days.

6

Resurgence

*O*n December 8, 1776, the army arrived in New-town, Pennsylvania, battered and weary from the long retreat across New Jersey. The Delaware River, a broad and icy barrier, now separated General Washington's forces from the pursuing British. It was here, amidst the chill of winter and the mounting despair, that Washington and his officers regrouped. The atmosphere at camp was fraught with worry. The men were hungry and worn, and the question of what came next hung heavy over them.

Washington understood the gravity of their situation. The Continental Army was dwindling, with enlistments set to expire at the end of the year. Morale was sinking under repeated defeats, and rumors of desertion spread through the ranks. Supplies were scarce, and the army's ability to hold together, let alone strike a blow against the British, seemed uncertain. Yet, Washington saw that inaction was not an option. To survive the winter, the revolution needed more than survival. We needed a victory.

In the days before Christmas, Washington resolved to act. By December 23, the decision had been made. The plan was audacious and carried tremendous risk. However, it also held the promise of revitalizing the faltering cause. Washington's target was the Hessian garrison stationed in Trenton, New Jersey, a town on the opposite bank of the Delaware River.

Trenton was not chosen lightly. The Hessians, German soldiers hired to help the British, led by Col. Johann Rall, were a formidable enemy, but they were one Washington believed he could overcome. Reports from scouts and spies described a garrison that had grown complacent. They had faced no significant threats and, with Christmas approaching, were likely to let down their guard. The timing of the attack was deliberate. Washington intended to strike on Christmas night, catching the enemy at their most vulnerable.

The town's location also made it a strategic prize. Situated along critical roads and supply routes, Trenton was a linchpin in the British and Hessian control of New Jersey. Capturing it would disrupt their operations and force them to reconsider their regional movements. A victory would also secure the Delaware

River crossings, allowing Washington to consolidate his position and plan future campaigns.

However, it was more than strategy that drove Washington to this decision. He knew his men needed a reason to believe in the cause and envision victory. The defeats of the past months had left the army on the verge of collapse, and the hope of a better outcome was slipping away. Success at Trenton could inspire soldiers to reenlist, rally recruits to the cause, and send a message to Congress and the American people that the fight was far from over.

Washington's plan was a gamble because it involved crossing the icy Delaware River at night on Christmas, catching Hessian forces off guard. The risks included severe weather, logistical challenges, and the morale of his poorly equipped, exhausted troops. Failure would have been disastrous for the Continental Army's survival and the revolutionary cause. But he was prepared to take it. The preparations began in earnest. Boats were gathered, provisions secured, and the army steeled itself for the challenge ahead. As the storm clouds gathered over the Delaware, we prepared to march, our spirits bolstered by the promise of redemption. Washington had decided to shift the momentum, and Trenton would be where he staked the revolution's future.

The plan was complex and involved coordinated

attacks from three directions. Brigadier General John Cadwalader would cross the river south of Bristol, Pennsylvania, at Dunks Ferry and move north toward Bordentown. Attacking the British garrison stationed there would impede the British from sending reinforcements. Brigadier General James Ewing would take his forces across the river at the Trenton Ferry and seize the bridge over Assunpink Creek to prevent enemy troops from escaping. Washington himself would lead the main force, crossing the river about nine miles north of Trenton and splitting into two groups for a predawn assault, with one group attacking from the north under Major General Nathanael Greene and the other from the south under Major General John Sullivan.

The biting wind cut through my ragged uniform as we trudged along the icy road toward Bristol, each step a battle against the cold. I was part of Nixon's regiment, which consisted of around 150 strong men under the command of Colonel Daniel Hitchcock. Our brigade was just one part of General Cadwalader's unit, a crucial piece of Washington's strategy.

The journey was grueling. The roads were a treacherous mix of ice and ruts, and many of us were without proper shoes, our feet wrapped in rags to ward off frostbite. Blood stained the snow as we marched, our makeshift coverings proving little protection against the sharp, frozen ground.

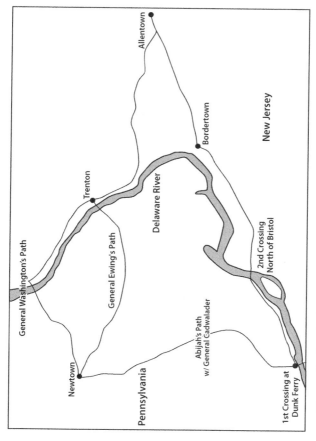

Figure 6 - On the March: Abijah's Movements at the Battle of Trenton

When we finally reached Dunks Ferry, the conditions only worsened. The river was a chaotic expanse of floating ice, and the wind howled uncompromisingly. Despite the harsh weather, General Cadwalader was determined to press on. He ordered more than six hundred foot soldiers, including my unit, to cross.

As we boarded the boats, the cold seeped through every layer of clothing, chilling us to the bone. The crossing itself was a harrowing ordeal. The river was difficult to navigate because it was full of ice. Our boats landed on an ice floe about 150 yards from the shore. We disembarked cautiously, the ice creaking ominously under our weight, and we could sense the water flowing underneath.

With our breath fogging in the frigid air, we moved inland, feeling the sting of the wind on our faces. But soon, word reached us that the boats carrying Cadwalader's artillery had been swept downstream. Without the artillery, continuing the mission was impossible. General Cadwalader made the difficult decision to call off the crossing until daylight, not wanting to split his forces and risk isolation. This setback underscored the strategic importance of the Delaware River, as it was a key obstacle for both the Continental Army and the British forces.

Receiving the order to fall back was met with mixed feelings. We had come so far and endured so much, yet we understood the necessity of staying united. Reluctantly, we made our way back to the boats. As we crossed the river once more, I couldn't help but feel a deep sense of frustration and exhaustion. The river seemed to mock us, its icy grip reminding us of the harsh reality of war.

Back on the other side, we regrouped and waited for daylight, our spirits dampened but not broken. The night was long, the cold was unforgiving, and the struggle was far from over. This failed attempt was just another chapter in our fight for freedom. Though the Delaware River had forced us to retreat for now, our unwavering drive to continue, despite the odds, showcased our strength and inspired all who witnessed our struggle.

Word soon reached us that General Washington had successfully crossed the Delaware and achieved a stunning victory against the Hessians in Trenton. The news spread like wildfire, rekindling our determination. It proved that victory was possible even in the face of overwhelming challenges.

On December 27, we attempted the crossing again, about a mile north of Bristol. The air was just as cold, the river just as treacherous, but our ranks had a renewed purpose. With the lessons learned from our previous attempt, we moved cautiously but deliberately. The rest of Cadwalader's brigade followed, and we reached the other side without incident.

The march to Bordentown on the twenty-eighth

was a grueling trek. Each step was a struggle, but the thought of the mission ahead kept us moving. When we finally arrived, we were met with disappointing news: The British had retreated to Allentown, about eight miles away. It was discouraging, but there was no time for despair. We immediately set our sights on Allentown and began the march.

The journey was arduous, the landscape a blur of snow and ice, but we pressed on with a singular focus. We reached Allentown, only to find it deserted. Again, the British had moved on, leaving us with nothing but their empty encampments. Frustration bubbled within the ranks. Still, we had reached our desired location, so we settled in and waited for new orders.

We remained in Allentown for several days. These days were a mix of restless waiting and constant vigilance. The cold was merciless, seeping into our bones, but we endured, driven by the hope of turning the tide in our favor. We fortified our position, tended to our wounds, and prepared for whatever lay ahead. But amidst the hardships, the camaraderie among the men, the shared stories, rations, and the burdens of war fortified our unity and created a strong bond that held us together as soldiers of the Continental Army.

The thought of home lingered as I sat beneath the gray winter sky, my fingers numb before I even picked up the quill. My family's faces came to me—my mother at the hearth, her hands busy with the tasks that never ceased; Jacob, just two, curious and full of small explorations that made up his days; my brothers, likely stretching themselves thin, helping Father keep the farm running in my absence. I wondered how the land had fared through the year, whether the harvest had been enough to sustain them, and if the roof still held against the weather. These thoughts gnawed at me more than the long march or the piercing cold.

Writing a letter felt like reaching across a gulf I wasn't sure could be crossed. Supplies were scarce, and even the ink and paper that cost me a small portion of my ration were bartered away to a fellow soldier who had kept them hidden. The paper was rough, its edges frayed, and the lines from my hurried hand were uneven when I finally folded it. Each word felt heavy, and I wrote sparingly, knowing the space was finite.

The letter was, therefore, brief. I told them I was alive and safe enough, offering what encouragement I could. I asked after their well-being, after the farm, after Jacob, and I kept the true weight of my struggles from them. There was no need to share details about the cold nights spent leaning against my musket for warmth. They had burdens enough of their own. Instead, I shaped myself in words as a soldier who held firm, even if the truth was far less steady.

When the ink dried, I folded the letter carefully and marked it with our name. Finding a way to send it home was no simple matter. I placed it with a messenger heading north, who swore to carry it as far as the nearest town where the name would be known. I knew it would travel slowly, passing from hand to hand, with no promise it would arrive. Still, as the letter left my hand, it gave me a sense of solace. Even if delayed or lost, sending it carried the hope that it might one day reach them, letting them know I had not been lost to the war.

As the new year dawned, there was a palpable sense of anticipation among us soldiers of the Continental Army. We knew that the coming days would bring new challenges and opportunities. Our failed crossings and the pursuit by the British united us by a common purpose and a stubborn will. The struggle for freedom was far from over, but as we stood ready in Allentown, we knew we were part of something much larger than ourselves. We were shaping history. The crossing of the Delaware, the bitter marches, and the endless cold were all part of our journey. But as the new year brought a fresh start, we faced the future with steadfast fortitude, ready to fight for the liberty we desperately sought. It seemed like there were no alternatives and no sense in giving up

Like many other men, my enlistment was about

to expire on December 31. However, General Washington appealed to the men by offering a ten-dollar bounty if we extended our service for one more month, which most of us accepted. On January 1, Captain Thompson was promoted to major, leaving us our second-in-command, Lieutenant William Toogood, who was soon promoted to captain as our company commander.

On that same day, we received new orders. Washington had learned that a British army of eight thousand men in Princetown, led by Cornwallis, was moving to attack Trenton. From Allentown, we hastily moved to the south bank of Assunpink Creek near the bridge that allowed traffic into Trenton, forming earthworks and preparing for a defensive battle.

Our situation was dreadful. We were trapped between the Delaware River and the advancing British army, with our boats over four miles away. The cold gnawed at our bones, and the knowledge of the impending British assault hung over us like a dark cloud. On the night of January 2, Washington made a bold decision. Under the cover of darkness, he ordered a surprise attack on Princetown, allowing us to move without the British becoming aware of our plans.

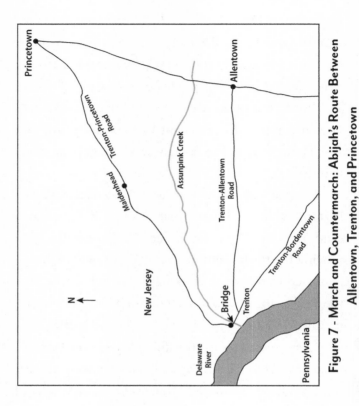

Figure 7 - March and Countermarch: Abijah's Route Between Allentown, Trenton, and Princetown

We left a small group of comrades behind to maintain cooking fires, creating the illusion that we were reinforcing our positions. They also made noise as if the entire army were still present. The flickering flames cast long shadows, masking our departure as the rest of our unit advanced cautiously toward Princetown. To muffle the sound of our movement, we wrapped the horses' hooves in cloth and covered the wagon and cannon wheels with straw. Taking a route that bypassed known locations containing enemy sentries, we chose lesser-used paths to avoid detection. Silenced by these precautions, the night was eerily quiet. Only the faint crunch of snow beneath our feet could be heard as we moved through the darkness. The tension of our mission heightened every sense.

It is only about nine miles, as the crow flies from Trenton to Princetown, but we marched almost twenty miles to escape the British clutches going back through Allentown. At about eight in the morning, having followed Quaker Road to Sawmill Road, we found ourselves just south of Princetown, and a skirmish erupted with British troops stationed there. The crack of musket fire and the shouts of commands filled the air. Our valor shone as we fought, every man aware of the stakes. The British were tough and well-trained, putting up staunch resistance. We found ourselves in close quarters, muskets and bayonets clashing, the air thick with smoke and shouts. It felt like we were on the brink, struggling against their disciplined lines. Every step was precarious on the frozen ground, and losing track of the overall objective in the confusion was easy. We fought with everything we had, pushing forward through the British defenses.

Eventually, we gained control of Princetown. The British began to retreat, and a brief but exhilarating cheer rose among our ranks. However, our victory was short-lived. The sounds of our battle had reached Cornwallis's ears, prompting him to gather his forces and march swiftly in our direction.

It was not long before we could hear General Cornwallis's troops coming from Trenton. The British reinforcements arrived faster than we anticipated, and for a moment it felt like the battle might be lost. The pressure was immense, and we were being pushed back. The situation grew desperate, and we were fighting for our lives.

We faced a daunting challenge. Our forces were worn to the bone, having had no respite for two grueling days and nights. Exhaustion threatened to overtake us. Just when our future seemed dim, a glimmer of hope emerged. General Sullivan arrived with American reinforcements, turning the tide of the battle.

With renewed strength and numbers, we managed to hold our ground. The arrival of Sullivan's troops had bolstered our spirits. Gradually, we pushed the British back, our combined forces proving too much for them. With Princetown secured, Cornwallis saw the futility of further attacks and decided to retreat, moving his army to New Brunswick for the winter.

As the British withdrew, a sense of hard-won triumph washed over us. We had faced incredible odds and emerged victorious. The journey had been long and filled with hardship, but we had proven our mettle. The winter ahead would be harsh, but we reveled in our current success. The crossing of the Delaware, the long marches, and the brutal battles had all led to this moment. We had made history, and though the struggle for freedom continued, this victory was a beacon of hope in our fight for independence.

Recognizing the need to shelter our troops from the harsh winter, General Washington strategically relocated our army to Morristown, where he would set up winter quarters. Our path involved a series of deliberate movements designed to avoid British forces and maximize our strategic advantages. As we marched toward Morristown, we crossed the Millstone River and took defensive action by destroying the bridge over the Millstone River near Kingstown. With that obstacle created, we marched northward to Somerset Court House in Somerville. Our arrival there was late in the day, well after the sun had set. Exhaustion weighed heavily on us.

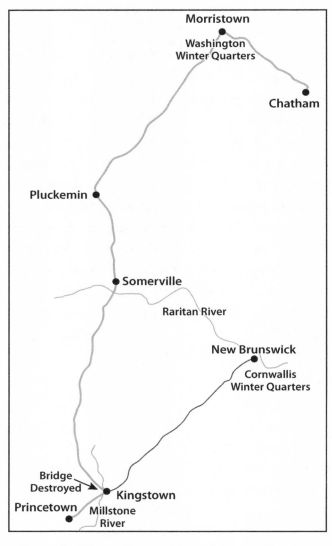

Figure 8 - Winter Quarters: Princetown to Chatham

We resumed our journey the following day, setting our sights on Pluckemin. In a commendable move, General Washington granted us a well-earned day of rest on that Sunday, January 5. Then, as the new week dawned, we continued our northward march toward Morristown, a place that would soon become our winter haven.

Once we arrived in Morristown, Washington stationed my unit near Chatham as a forward outpost used to provide early warning in case of an attack. It was near Chatham that I ended my enlistment, eager to return to the hamlet at Green River and reunite with my family. The past year had been uncertain and challenging, but I had survived and played a part in a pivotal chapter of the American Revolution.

The attacks on Trenton and Princetown significantly boosted our morale. These victories showed us we could succeed even when faced with formidable odds. The victories also inspired a sense of hope and commitment to the cause among existing soldiers, fostering a more profound belief in our ability to win the war. Moreover, these victories had a positive impact on recruiting new soldiers. The successful attacks demonstrated that the American forces were a viable and determined fighting force, attracting recruits inspired by the recent triumphs and the opportunity to join a cause gaining momentum.

7

Rest and Relaxation

*A*fter receiving my discharge at Chatham, New Jersey, I traveled by foot to Green River. Being home with my family brought joy and relief. I needed a rest from the fighting. When I arrived, I discovered my parents were struggling on the farm. Cash was challenging to come by. Farmers had little of it and bartered for their needed provisions. Having received the bounty for extending my enlistment and my back pay of six dollars a month for serving in December 1776 and January 1777, I had a few dollars, most of which I gave to my family to help. It was a small but significant sacrifice for the cause.

At eighteen, on the verge of reaching nineteen, I stood as a product of revolutionary origins. I had evolved into a soldier, shaped by the toil of hard work and the burning zeal of patriotism. One tale of my strength spoke of the day I carried three burlap bags of rock salt up three flights of stairs in a single load, an impossible feat for most that proved my incredible might.

I remember, as if it were yesterday, when I realized I had a natural talent for strength challenges. I became a legend among my friends and family for it. Shortly after arriving home, I went to Nobletown for a wagonload of rock salt with my two older brothers, James and Asa, and my sister Bethia's husband, Ephraim Bronson. Rock salt had many uses. It served as a vital preservative, mainly used to preserve food like meat and fish by inhibiting bacterial growth and preventing spoilage. Additionally, it flavored food and had various household applications, such as curing leather and making brine. It also played a role in some traditional medicine practices and was used in livestock care to provide essential minerals.

It was a brutally cold winter morning, and we were unloading the shipment of rock salt. Each burlap bag weighed about one hundred pounds, and we had to haul them up three flights of stairs to the barn's storage area. It was grueling work that tested our endurance and strength to the limit.

A thought struck me as I stood facing the mountain of bags: Why not carry more than one at a time? The idea seemed preposterous initially, but the challenge ignited my unyielding drive. I decided to take as many bags as possible in a single trip, a solution that seemed to push the boundaries of possibility.

I picked up the first bag, the coarse salt shifting around as I hefted it onto my shoulder. Then I picked up the second bag, balancing it carefully. My fellow workers watched in silence, their expressions mixed with curiosity and doubt. Lifting the third bag, I could feel the strain in my muscles, the weight pressing down on me like a tangible force. Realizing I needed help, I called out to my coworkers. "Hey, can you guys help me out? Place the third bag on me," I said.

They looked at me, their faces a mix of surprise and admiration, but they didn't hesitate to lend a hand. One lifted the third bag and carefully placed it on top of the others, ensuring it was balanced. With all three bags of rock salt weighing about three hundred pounds, I took my first step toward the stairs. The weight was almost overwhelming, but I focused on maintaining my balance and controlling my breathing. Each step was deliberate, every movement precise. The stairs creaked under the weight of my burden as I climbed them.

By the time I reached the second floor, my body was screaming for relief, but I pushed through the pain. My coworkers' murmurs of disbelief and encouragement echoed behind me. On the third-floor landing, I finally sat the last bag down, my entire body trembling from the effort.

The room erupted in cheers and applause. I had done it. I had carried three hundred pounds of rock salt up three flights of stairs in a single load. I stood there, drenched in sweat, catching my breath and feeling proud. It was a moment that spoke of my incredible strength and willpower, a story that would be told among my peers for years to come.

As my heart rate slowed and my muscles began to relax, I thought about the importance of physical endurance, not just for moments like these but for the countless challenges life had in store. One of the challenges I met regularly during the war was wrestling matches.

Wrestling matches were a regular occurrence within the ranks of the Continental Army during the American Revolutionary War, even though the sport was officially forbidden. As soldiers, we sought various forms of leisure and physical activity to alleviate the rigors of military life and foster camaraderie. Wrestling allowed us to test our strength and skill, forging stronger bonds with our fellow soldiers. Despite its prohibition, the sport was irresistible, though there were good reasons for the ban. Wrestling could easily lead to injuries, sprains, bruises, and even broken bones, which could sideline a soldier and strain our limited medical resources. It also encouraged rowdiness and the occasional flare-up of tempers, which was a potential threat to the discipline and unity crucial for an effective army. Nevertheless, these contests played an essential role in elevating our spirits and provided much-needed entertainment in our moments of respite at camp. I was proud to excel as a champion wrestler in my regiment, carrying my prowess onto the battlefield and into the taverns, where we sought brief refuge from the harsh realities of war.

It was a cold and wet night in January 1777 at Hatch's Tavern just outside Nobletown. The air was thick with the scent of ale and the smoke from the fireplace. I sat at a corner table, nursing my drink and keeping a wary eye on the room. My worn tricorn hat shaded my face, but my gaze was intense, scanning for any sign of trouble.

Four Tories from Kinderhook had gathered at the bar, huddled together, sneering and mocking the Patriots. They laughed about our losses and belittled our efforts, thinking themselves superior in every way. My grip tightened around my tankard, but I held my tongue. I wasn't looking for a fight, but I wasn't about to let them insult us without consequence. The insults continued, growing more malicious, until one of them, a young man with a fanatical gleam in his eye, leaned in and hissed, "I say we teach any Patriot we find a lesson they won't forget."

I felt my patience snap. I stood up slowly, my chair scraping against the wooden floor, drawing the attention of the entire tavern. I walked over to the bar, my eyes locked on the Tories. A burly Tory turned, eyeing me with contempt. "Look what we have here, boys. A rebel dog comes to bark at us."

Before I could respond, one of the Tories swung a punch at me. I turned my head and leaned back, my reflexes honed by months of fighting, as I felt his fist move the air across my face. I countered with a swift uppercut, catching him under the chin and sending him sprawling.

The tavern erupted into chaos. The burly Tory lunged at me, but I sidestepped, grabbing a nearby stool and swinging it with all my might. The stool shattered against his side, and he crumpled to the floor, gasping for breath.

The young fanatic and the other Tory advanced together. I backed up, grabbing a half-full tankard from a nearby table and hurling its contents into the Tory's face. Blinded and sputtering, he staggered, giving me the opening I needed. I grabbed him by the arm and spun him overhead with a roar, feeling the strain in my muscles as he thrashed helplessly. With a final grunt, I tossed him into the fireplace. He landed in a crash, sending sparks flying and the flames roaring higher.

The young fanatic, undeterred, pulled a knife from his belt and lunged at me with a wild cry. I dodged, grabbing his wrist and twisting it until the knife clattered to the floor. With a mighty shove, I sent him stumbling backward. I then grabbed him by the collar and the belt, hoisting him off the ground. I carried him to the door, kicked it open with my foot, and hurled him outside. He landed in the mud with a splat, then scrambled to his feet and fled into the night.

Breathing heavily, I looked around the tavern. The patrons had fallen silent, watching the scene with wide eyes. I straightened my tricorn hat and glared at the remaining Tories. The Tories groaned and muttered curses, but none dared to rise. I nodded, satisfied, and walked back to my table. I sat down, my back to the wall, and resumed my drink, my eyes never leaving the fallen Tories. The tavern slowly returned to its usual clamor, but the message was clear: The Patriots were not to be underestimated.

A few days passed, and I thought the incident was behind me. But those Tories returned, this time with a couple more men in tow. They found me at the tavern, and this time they overwhelmed me. They beat me mercilessly, tied me up with ropes, and dragged me outside. They threw me into the tavern's ash house with a cruel laugh, closed the door, and latched it. I heard them return to the tavern to celebrate their so-called victory, their cruel cackles ringing in my ears.

I lay there in the dark, pain coursing through my body, thinking my end had come. But the future held other plans. I heard the door creak open. An Indigenous woman stood looking down at me, her eyes wide with concern. She had heard my groans and, risking her own life, came to help me. "Shh," she whispered, cutting my bindings with a small knife. "You live."

She helped me to my feet, supporting my weight as we slipped out of the ash house. We crept through the woods, her presence a beacon of hope. She tended to my wounds, and with her help, I managed to escape the Tories' grasp.

I never learned her name, but I owe her my life. Her bravery and kindness reminded me that there is always hope and unexpected allies, even in the darkest times. So, never underestimate the power of courage and compassion. They can turn the tide of events in the most remarkable ways.

It was February now, and I was healed and well-rested. The news of the British attack and victory at Fort McIntosh had reached my ears, and the call to duty echoed loudly in my heart. Though I felt a pang of worry about leaving the farm, I knew it was in capable hands with James and Asa. They would keep things running smoothly, and their duties with the Albany militia weren't so frequent as to pull them away too often.

When I told my family I was signing up with the Continentals again, their faces spoke before their voices could. My mother's hands stilled for a moment, resting on her apron, her fingers trembling slightly before she folded them. She didn't protest, not directly. She had always been proud of my service, but there was a weariness in her eyes, a weight that hadn't been there before the war began. Her voice was soft but firm when it came, telling me only to come back, whole and alive, if I could.

My father and brothers were quiet, their glances heavy with understanding. My father was disappointed. The farm demanded more than his absence with the militia could spare. Crops needed tending, livestock feeding, and fences mending, and his sons, who also had militia duty, were often called at the same time as he. Still, he trusted us to try, just as he trusted his daughters and my mother to carry the weight of the household in his absence. Asa and James had already taken on more than their share, keeping the farm running while I was away. They hadn't complained, not once, but I knew the strain I was leaving behind for them to shoulder. They didn't argue about my choice; they knew the cause was greater than any of us. But I could see in the set of their jaws and the stiffness in their hands that they wished it didn't have to be this way.

The younger one, Jacob, especially didn't understand fully. At two years old, he clung to my leg, his tiny hands gripping my worn trousers as though he could keep me from going. Hulda tried to distract him, brushing the curls from his face and whispering reassurances, though I could see the tears gathering in her eyes. She'd watched her father leave for the militia, and now she was watching her brother go, uncertain if he'd ever return.

The farm itself seemed to mourn my decision. The tools leaning against the barn and the fields half-covered in the snow reminded me of the work I was leaving undone. The fences would sag further, the plow might rust, and the harvest would be harder without my hands. Yet, the pull to the war was stronger than even that sense of duty to the land.

They didn't try to stop me. No one begged me to stay. They all knew why I had to go, why this fight mattered. But their silence spoke volumes about the sacrifice that they were making too. My mother held me a little longer than usual when we said goodbye, her arms firm despite trembling. Asa's slap on my shoulder felt heavier than it should have, and Hulda's whispered prayer followed me as I stepped out the door.

I carried their worry and their pride with me, an invisible burden that felt heavier than the pack on my back. It was challenging to leave them again, but the cause pulled me forward. Still, I promised myself I would return to them, no matter what it took.

Reassured, I gathered my belongings and left the warmth of my family once more to embark on a new chapter. I sought out Captain Toogood's company this time, finding them in Middle Brook, New Jersey, about four miles west of Somerville. I enlisted for three years without hesitation.

8

The Tide Turns

I arrived in late February and spent March with the unit in New Jersey. By April, General Washington had ordered my unit to move to Peekskill, New York, where the regiment was assigned to Major General Israel Putnam's division, part of Major General Philip Schuyler's Northern Army.

Peekskill, New York, was a strategically important location near the Hudson Highlands. It controlled access to the Hudson River, which was a critical waterway for transportation and communication during the war. Washington needed to maintain control of the Hudson River to prevent the British from dividing the colonies and to protect the vital supply lines along the river. Washington wanted to ensure that this area was adequately protected, as controlling the Highlands would make it more difficult for the British to navigate the Hudson River.

The looming threat of a British invasion from Canada under Major General John Burgoyne's command weighed heavily on our minds. It was not long in coming, for on July 5, Burgoyne captured Fort Ticonderoga, and the American commander, Major General Arthur St. Clair, was forced to abandon the fort. He and his men narrowly escaped, and their supplies remained intact.

On July 8, we boarded transports in Peekskill and sailed up the Hudson River, finally arriving in Albany on July 12. My regiment, comprising about five hundred men, was dispatched to Fort Ann, roughly fifty miles north of Albany. Our mission was clear: delay Burgoyne's advance and buy precious time for the Americans to prepare for battle.

Our journey followed the Hudson River's western side until we reached Fort Edward, where we encountered a portage around the falls. Unbeknownst to us then, a party of two thousand Iroquois had taken control of Fort Ann. As we moved forward, a small unit of our own was attacked by four hundred of these natives near the fort on July 21. Lacking the resources for a full-scale assault, we halted our march just a few miles south of Fort Ann and immediately began our delaying tactics.

We burned sawmills, destroyed roads, felled trees into the navigable waters, and rounded up cattle, driving them toward Albany, all the while sabotaging any potential sources of supply for Burgoyne's army. As we retreated, we ensured that every bridge crossed was left in ruins on our march back to Albany. By the end of August, we were back in Albany, where we learned that Major General Horatio Gates had replaced General Schuyler as the commander of the Northern Army.

Despite our valiant efforts, Burgoyne's army continued its ruthless southward march. The atrocities committed by Burgoyne's Iroquois allies against noncombatants, particularly women, spurred the region's populace into action. Men from towns far and wide rallied to the cause, including my original militia unit, the Albany County Militia, which my brother James served in.

With General Gates came the esteemed Major General Benedict Arnold and his men, further bolstering our forces. We were now a formidable army of seven thousand, encamped on a high bluff known as Bemis Heights, located on the west side of the Hudson River just south of Saratoga. The Hudson River fortified this strategic position on our right flank and General Arnold's two thousand men on our left.

The pivotal moment came on September 19, when Burgoyne sent several units forward to attack General Arnold's left flank. Instead of remaining in his

defensive position, Arnold chose to launch an audacious attack. The battle raged for three hours, with the
field changing hands multiple times. When darkness
fell, our units withdrew to Bemis Heights, leaving the
field to the British. The casualties were grim, with six
hundred British soldiers killed or captured and over
three hundred American lives lost. My regiment, held
in reserve, could only watch in awe and horror.

Both sides remained encamped for the following
three weeks, the tension palpable. Let me tell you,
the British were in a real bind during that time. Their
supply lines were stretched so thin you could almost
see through them, and they were running out of everything: food, ammunition, you name it. To make
matters worse, we Americans had control of the surrounding areas, so they couldn't quickly get what they
needed.

During this time, the British built three redoubts
to hold their ground. These redoubts were well-built,
with earth and timber, and strategically positioned.
They hoped these defenses would keep us at bay and
protect their troops from an assault.

The first redoubt, named Breymann, was on the
right flank, protecting their line from any attacks from
that direction. The second, Balcarres, was a bit further
south, about two or three hundred yards, more cen-
trally located, and served as a strong point in their

defense. The third, the Great Redoubt, was on the left, guarding a potential approach from the Hudson. The British hoped these redoubts would give them a fighting chance to hold out, especially since they were low on supplies and facing increasing pressure from our forces.

But, despite these fortifications, they were still in a tough spot. They tried to stretch their resources and defend against us, but those redoubts could only do so much. It was clear to us that they were getting desperate, and even with those defenses, they couldn't stay there indefinitely without reinforcements or more supplies.

On October 7, sensing his predicament and knowing his options were depleted, Burgoyne launched an attack. Once again, our regiment was held in reserve. Burgoyne sent his men out from the Balcarres Redoubt to attack our lines. The British came at us hard, forcing us to fall back initially. They had the upper hand for a while, pushing us away from their defensive positions.

We had two entire brigades there. Brigadier General Ebenezar Learned's Massachusetts Brigade attacked the British positions, including the Balcarres Redoubt, and Brigadier General Enoch Poor's New Hampshire Brigade also engaged in the assault. Colonel Daniel Morgan's sharpshooters were critical in harassing the British defenders. His men targeted officers and key personnel, contributing significantly to the disarray among the British forces.

The British were pushed back into the redoubt. We fought hard, and the British pushed back just as hard. The redoubt was well-fortified, and even though the Americans got close, they couldn't break through. The British held their ground, forcing us to pull back from Balcarres.

However, General Arnold, who was without a command at that time due to a dispute with General Gates, was not about to give up. Despite not having formal command, he took matters into his own hands. He noticed Breymann's Redoubt, a minor position held by a group of Hessians, was vulnerable. This redoubt was a few hundred yards northwest of Balcarres, and Arnold saw an opportunity.

Arnold, leading the charge, swung around to the southern end of Breymann's Redoubt. His energy was infectious, like a man possessed, as he rallied everyone around him. Morgan's riflemen and the other units followed his lead and attacked Breymann's position. It was a furious assault, with the sounds of musket fire cracking and bayonets clashing. Arnold was right in the thick of it, fighting with a tenacity that inspired all who saw him.

Our troops managed to sweep around and hit them from the south. The Hessians fought back, but they were overwhelmed by our attack. Arnold was fanatical, urging the men on, and finally, Breymann's Redoubt was captured. It was a significant blow to the British as their entire right flank collapsed. Arnold's bold maneuver and the brutal fighting of our troops paid off.

With Breymann's Redoubt captured, the British positions were significantly weakened. The next day, Burgoyne pulled his men back to Saratoga. Due to the driving rain, they could not escape farther north since the roads were impassable.

By October 10, our unit had advanced up to a point where the Fish Kill emptied into the Hudson River. On October 11, my unit received orders to attack at dawn. A dense fog enveloped the battlefield as we advanced along Fish Kill. Unbeknownst to us, the main force of Burgoyne's army, armed with twenty-seven pieces of artillery, lay concealed within the mist. Brigadier General John Glover's brigade, following closely, discovered a British deserter who revealed the danger that awaited us. Glover urgently informed Nixon, who swiftly halted our unit. The fog lifted in a cruel twist of events, exposing both sides. The British artillery opened fire, claiming several lives and narrowly sparing Nixon from a cannonball that damaged his eyesight and hearing. We retreated swiftly, taking our dead and wounded with us.

Men continued to pour into the patriot units,

swelling our numbers. Among those called to action were the men of the Albany County Militia, including the 9th Regiment. Unknown to me then, this regiment included my two brothers, Asa and James, who answered the call to defend their home and country. By October 14, Burgoyne and his army were entirely encircled, their supply lines severed. On October 17, surrender became inevitable, a victory forged by the collective efforts of countless men like my brothers, whose contributions I would only learn of later.

Following Burgoyne's capitulation, our unit was ordered back to Albany. The town's residents billeted us in their homes for the winter. By November, we transitioned from General Putnam's division to Major General Alexander McDougall, while Nixon took leave until June 1778.

Rumors of an invasion of Canada circulated, but by March 1778, the plan had been abandoned. In June, Nixon returned, and we were relocated to White Plains, New York. By October, Nixon sought another leave, and Colonel John Greaton assumed brigade command. The winter of 1778 and 1779 saw us stationed around New York City as the war's focus shifted south.

By the spring of 1779, we were stationed at one of the most crucial spots in the war effort, West Point.

West Point wasn't the mighty fortress you might picture today, but we knew its importance even then. The place sat on the Hudson River, controlling access and keeping the British from splitting the colonies.

Our duties there were a mix of grueling work and constant vigilance. We spent much time fortifying the place, building and maintaining redoubts, batteries, and defenses. It was challenging to haul earth and timber, dig trenches, and set up cannon positions. We knew that if the British ever decided to make a serious move, those defenses would be our first and last line of defense.

A steadfast leader, Captain Toogood kept our spirits up and ensured we stayed sharp. We couldn't let our guard down for a moment. Patrols and reconnaissance became routine. We'd head out and scout the area, keeping an eye on the British and ensuring our supply lines stayed clear. It wasn't glamorous work, but it was vital. We had to know what the enemy was up to and be ready to respond immediately.

There were a few tense moments, especially when rumors of British movements would reach us. We'd double our patrols, sometimes skirmishing with Loyalist militias or British scouts. These weren't significant battles, but they kept us on our toes and reminded us that we were always in danger. We knew that if the British managed to take West Point, they'd have a chokehold on the Hudson River, which could be disastrous for our cause.

The work was ceaseless, and the conditions weren't easy. We were always short on supplies, and the following winter was severe. Despite the hardships, there was a strong sense of duty among us. Captain Toogood and the other officers ensured we understood our mission's importance. We knew we were guarding a critical point, and that gave us a sense of purpose.

One incident stands out. There was a day when a British force was rumored to be moving toward the river. It was a false alarm, but it showed how dangerous things could get at any point. The British knew the value of West Point, just as we did, and they kept us on edge.

Looking back, that time at West Point was challenging but also a point of pride. We knew we were playing a part in something significant that could change the war's course and contribute to a favorable outcome. We weren't just soldiers; we were defenders of a vital stronghold. And while we didn't see large-scale battles, the daily grind of fortifying and guarding that position was just as crucial to our ultimate success.

That's how it was with Captain Toogood's company in 1779. We weren't always in the thick of the fight, but we were always ready, always watching, and always working to ensure that West Point would hold when the time came. And hold it we did, through all the trials and tribulations of that year.

9

Imprisoned

In February of 1780, my three-year enlistment finally ended, and I headed back home to Green River. As I
reached my beloved Green River, I learned of a significant change involving my old company commander,
Joseph Thompson, who had guided me through battles
and hardships. He had been promoted to lieutenant
colonel and entrusted with a regimental command. His
new post was at Joseph Young's farm, near the cross-
roads known as Four Corners in Westchester County,
a perilous area between British-controlled New York
City and American-held territory, commonly called
"no man's land."

Lieutenant Colonel Thompson had about 250
men under his command. The area he was guarding
stretched about ten to fifteen miles, give or take, depending on how many men were available and how
critical certain roads and settlements were. His main

job was to keep the British from pushing further into Westchester County and to throw a wrench into their supply lines and scouting missions. It wasn't an easy task. Trying to cover that much ground with the number of troops he had was no small feat, especially with British raids and skirmishes constantly keeping them on edge.

Thompson got word that a British unit of five to six hundred men was bearing down on his location. When Thompson's men met the enemy in front of the Youngs' house, they were quickly surrounded, and panic set in for many of the soldiers who fled down the road. Some officers, including Thompson, and others fortified themselves inside the house, determined to hold off the British. But it wasn't to be. In no time, they surrendered and were taken as prisoners of war. To add to the tragedy, the British burned down Youngs' house.

There was little time to dwell on it. Captain Walter Vrooman came through town looking for volunteers to join Colonel John Harper's Regiment of Levies in Schenectady, and I did not hesitate. I enlisted for nine months without a second thought.

Under Captain Vrooman, we spent a few weeks in Schenectady before joining the First New York Regiment at Fort Stanwix in late March. Arriving there was a bit of a shock. Fort Stanwix faced a multitude of challenges. Situated in isolation from nearby settlements, it posed a difficult situation for men venturing out in small groups, especially as a continuous specter of native attacks loomed. Within the fort's confines, provisions were in short supply due to the considerable distance between the fort and Continental supply depots. This presented an ongoing logistical struggle to maintain adequate supplies.

After years of raids, supply shortages, sieges, and desertions, the morale of the 1st New York Regiment was lower than any unit I had ever seen. Court-martials were a daily affair as the men began to rebel. But when I thought I couldn't take the stress any longer, life had other plans.

Sir Frederick Haldimand, the British governor of Canada, heard of a bumper crop of grain in the Mohawk and Schoharie Valleys. Therefore, he sent an expedition under Lieutenant Colonel Sir John Johnson to raid the countryside and destroy the harvest to prevent our armies from using it. They gathered a force of about 750 men and set off from Montreal, sailing upriver to Lake Ontario and across it to British-held Fort Ontario. The fort is located where the Oswego River empties into Lake Ontario.

Using a flotilla of bateaux for transportation, Sir Johnson's men followed the Oswego River upstream to Oneida Lake. Afterward, they continued to an old palisade fort built by the French in 1756, a few miles south of the lake. There, they concealed some provisions and boats for their return trip, leaving a small detachment to guard the supplies.

News of this expedition reached the commander at Fort Stanwix, who promptly sent word to Governor George Clinton of New York. The governor dispatched Brigadier General Robert Van Rensselaer to gather eight hundred men and intercept Sir Johnson's forces. On October 17, General Van Rensselaer began his march to Fort Hunter. Arriving there on the eighteenth, he learned Sir Johnson's forces had already passed through. Continuing the march, General Van Rensselaer headed to Fultonville, arriving at midnight, prepared to engage the enemy.

The battle began on the morning of the nineteenth, and Sir John's men quickly faced overwhelming American forces. The British retreated, and General Van Rensselaer pursued them, eventually catching up with Sir Johnson near Jacob Klock's farm. Still, the day was almost over, and the cover of darkness saved Sir Johnson's men, allowing them to escape across the river.

But the story doesn't end there. General Van Rensselaer learned about Sir Johnson's planned route and their hidden boats and supplies near Lake Oneida from the prisoners he captured. So he dispatched a messenger to Fort Stanwix to send a detachment to destroy the enemy's supplies and boats before Sir Johnson and his men could reach them.

At the fort, the commander, Major James M. Hughes, stood before us, his eyes scanning the faces of the weary soldiers. A solemn hush hung in the air, and he asked for volunteers. Captain Vrooman, a brave and stubborn man, stepped forward without hesitation and offered to lead the unit. His determination was contagious, and it spread through the ranks like wildfire.

I stood there with only six weeks left on my current enlistment, but my resolve was unwavering. This daring raid, a striking act of foraging warfare, demanded a swift response. Sixty men volunteered, and I was one of them. Captain Vrooman took charge, and our detachment of volunteers wasted no time. We departed swiftly toward our destination, Oneida Lake.

As we ventured toward the Tuscarora Village of Canaseraga, one of our companions fell ill and could no longer keep pace with our determined march. Reluctantly, we left him behind, his future uncertain in the wilderness.

On October 23, 1780, we reached our destination, a few miles from where Canaseraga Creek flowed into Lake Oneida, and were met with the sight we had expected. Several boats and the surplus stores were under guard, but only about seven defenders were there. Luckily, they surrendered quickly to our overwhelming force. We began our work, destroying the supplies and sending the boats to the river's depths.

However, luck is an erratic wind, shifting direction when least expected. While we dined, blissfully unaware, Sir Johnson and his forces surrounded us. They had learned of our mission from the ailing soldier we left behind. In surprising events, Sir Johnson's forces captured all sixty of us without firing a single shot.

The British and their Indigenous allies were incensed by our audacious actions. Five brave comrades met a swift and unfortunate end, while a sixth was subjected to the brutal gauntlet. Promising his life if he survived, they bound his ankles and knees together and set him on a harrowing run through two rows of armed natives, all eager to strike a blow. Before he could reach the end, he was struck down, battered by cruel clubs, and then carried across the creek, where he was roasted alive.

These were no ordinary adversaries but members of the Turtle Clan, part of the Huron tribe. Their presence on the battlefield spoke of a people deeply rooted in tradition and survival. Their movements were swift and deliberate, honed by generations of conflict and adaptation. The Turtle Clan, like the rest of the Huron, carried the weight of their history into every encounter, their actions as much a defense of their identity as an act of war.

The Huron were no strangers to struggle. Displaced from their ancestral lands near Georgian Bay decades earlier, they had been scattered by pressure from the Haudenosaunee, a confederacy of six Indigenous nations, and the encroachment of European powers. Yet, they had not lost their sense of unity even in their dispersal. Among their clans, the Turtle stood as a symbol of endurance, their very name tied to creation stories that placed the turtle at the foundation of the world itself. This was not passive endurance but rather vigorously engaged willpower to hold onto what remained of their lands and their people, even as the tides of war threatened to swallow them.

The Turtle Clan's warriors carried more than weapons into battle. They bore the knowledge of their terrain, the echoes of their ancestors' wisdom, and the weight of their community's survival. Every arrow launched and every musket fired was an act of resilience and a statement that they would not vanish without a fight. Their tactics were sharp and calculated, using the forests as their shields and the rivers as their allies. During these tumultuous years, they fought not just to defend their allies, often the British, but to carve out a future amidst the chaos that colonial wars brought to their world.

Their resolve was mixed with sorrow and defiance, as if they carried the memories of all they had lost alongside their fire to protect what little they still had.

For the Turtle Clan and the Huron, survival was more than staying alive. It was about ensuring their culture, clans, and stories would continue, even if it meant facing foes like us on the battlefield. To commemorate their victory, the warriors carved the image of a turtle into the bark of a towering tree near the battlefield. This enduring mark, etched with care, served as a testament to their triumph and a reminder of their enduring strength and unity in the face of conflict.

Forced by our captors, we raised most of the boats we had sunk and repaired them to cross Lake Oneida, carrying the remnants of the supplies we had not destroyed. With Sir Johnson's forces retreating to Fort Ontario, we were compelled to make the arduous journey with them. After arriving at Fort Ontario, we were loaded onto boats with sails and transported to Montreal.

The journey by sail was cold and uncomfortable. The wind whipped across the lake, making the waters choppy and the air biting. We huddled together on the deck, trying to keep warm under the watchful eyes of the guards. The vast expanse of water stretched around us, a stark reminder of how far we were from home. As the days passed, the shoreline came into view, and we soon reached Montreal. The city was bustling, a mix of French and British influences, but we saw little of it. Our time there was brief; we were quickly assembled and forced to march eastward toward Fort Chambly, about fifteen miles away.

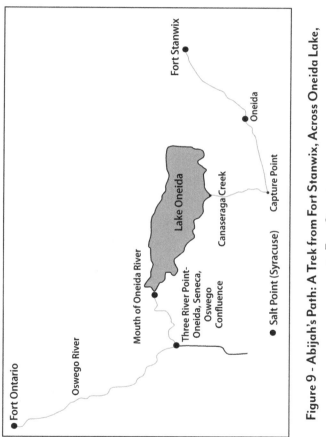

Figure 9 - Abijah's Path: A Trek from Fort Stanwix, Across Oneida Lake, to Fort Ontario

The march was grueling. The terrain was rough, a mix of forested areas and open land, and the temperature dropped steadily as we moved deeper into British territory. The soldiers kept us moving at a steady pace, their presence a constant reminder of our captivity. As we marched, the environment around us became increasingly stark. The trees stood bare, their leaves fallen, and the ground was hard with frost. The sky remained overcast, a dull gray that matched the mood of our group. I tried to focus on the landscape, taking in the sights and sounds, but the cold made it difficult to think of anything other than keeping moving. The thought of escape flickered briefly, but the harsh conditions and the soldiers' vigilance made it seem impossible.

Finally, we reached Fort Chambly. The fort's stone walls rose before us, imposing and impenetrable. The Richelieu River flowed nearby, its waters cold and unforgiving. The sight of the fort filled me with awe and dread. With its high and thick walls, it was clear this place was meant to withstand sieges. The river, which had been a route for trade and travel, now felt like a barrier, cutting us off from the outside world.

As we entered the fort, the heavy wooden gates closed behind us, sealing us from the world. Inside, the fort was bustling with activity. British soldiers moved about, preparing for the winter and maintaining the fort's defenses. The fort's stone construction, while sturdy, made the air cold and damp. The walls seemed to absorb the chill and radiate it back at us, a constant reminder of the harsh winter ahead.

The guards led the small group of us to our cell, a small, cramped room within the barracks. The floor was hard-packed earth, and the walls were thick stone, cold to the touch. A small, barred window let in only a sliver of pale light. The room was sparsely furnished with a thin layer of straw on the ground and a single, unused fireplace. The air was heavy with the smell of dampness and the presence of too many unwashed bodies in too small a space.

As we settled into our new reality, the routine of prison life began to set in. The guards were ever-present, ensuring we knew our place. The food was sparse and barely enough to sustain us, and the cold was unremitting. Each day blended into the next, marked only by our routine. The stone walls and barred windows became our world, a small, confined space within the vast landscape of Quebec. The fort's strategic importance to the British was of little comfort to us; it was simply our prison, a place we had to endure.

As I lay on the hard floor, staring up at the stone ceiling, I couldn't help but think of the journey that had brought me here. Fort Chambly stood as a symbol of British power, yet also a reminder of the harsh realities of war. My only hope was that this would not be the end of my journey and that, somehow, I would find a way back home. Until then, all I could do was endure, survive, and wait for a chance at freedom.

The cold, damp walls of my cell at Fort Chambly seemed to close around me as the days dragged on. It was late February in 1781, and the isolation of my imprisonment was starting to wear me down. Every day was a torture of monotony. The guards' shouts rudely awakened us. "Up! All up!" they would bark, their voices echoing through the dim room. We rose sluggishly, stiff from the cold and the constant ache of hunger. The guards counted us individually, ensuring no one had slipped away during the night. The thought of escape had crossed my mind more than once, but with the frigid winter outside and the high fortress walls, it seemed an impossible dream.

Once the roll call was complete, we were given our meager breakfast: a small piece of coarse bread and a soup ladle of thin gruel. It wasn't much, but it was all we had to fuel us through the long day. As I chewed the dry bread, I thought of home, my mother's hearty meals, and the warmth of our family hearth. It felt like a lifetime ago.

After breakfast, we were assigned our daily tasks. Some days, the guards put us to work chopping wood, which was grueling and oddly welcome, for it warmed us in a way nothing else could. We would be kept in-side during inclement weather. Those days would have us mending worn-out clothing and gear. It was tedious work, but it kept us busy and our minds occupied. As I worked, my thoughts often wandered to the past, the battles fought, and the friends lost. The camaraderie we shared in those moments of danger was something I missed dearly.

Lunch was scarcely different from breakfast. If we were lucky, it was another serving of gruel, slightly thicker this time, with perhaps a small bit of salted meat. The food was far from satisfying, but it was sustenance. We huddled together as we ate, sharing stories from home, dreams of freedom, and, occasionally, whispered plans of escape. Though the latter seemed more and more futile with each passing day, it gave us something to cling to, a spark of hope in the darkness.

As the afternoon waned, we were given some time to ourselves. This was both a blessing and a curse. The time stretched out, the silence occasionally broken by my fellow prisoners murmurs or the guards distant sounds. I often found myself staring out the small, barred window, watching the snow fall softly, the landscape a blanket of white. It was beautiful, yet it was a cruel reminder of our confinement.

The evening brought another scant meal and the final roll call of the day. As darkness settled, we were herded back into the barracks, the heavy door shut tight behind us, and the night stretched long and freezing. We tried to sleep, wrapped in whatever clothing and blankets we had, but it was never enough. The wind howled outside, and I lay awake, shivering, my thoughts racing. I thought of my family, the farm, and the life I had left behind. I wondered if I would ever see them again or if this winter fortress would be my end.

As the hours dragged on, I listened to the sounds around me: the soft breathing of the men, the occasional cough, and the rustle of someone turning over in their sleep. It was a restless night, like so many others. The cold was persistent, seeping into every bone and muscle. My stomach growled, and hunger was ever-present. But more than the physical discomfort, it was the uncertainty that gnawed at me, not knowing when or if this captivity would end.

Despite the overwhelming despair, a peculiar perseverance buoyed me. Whether it was the shared suffering, the bond forged with my fellow captives, or the faint, flickering hope of freedom, I cannot say. But it was enough to keep me waking each day, facing the monotony and hardship, and holding on to the belief that, somehow, I would endure this time at Fort Chambly and return to the life I once knew.

As the first light of dawn crept into the room,

I knew the cycle would begin anew, another day of cold, hunger, and survival. But I lay there, eyes closed, clutching my thin blanket. This was my life, but I vowed it wouldn't be forever. One day, I would be free again. One day, I would go home.

I was determined to defy my captors and reclaim my freedom. A small group of us huddled in a dim, cramped cell. Driven by desperation, we had been meticulously planning our escape for weeks. The concept was straightforward: elude the guards, cross the river, and disappear into the wilderness.

Getting past the guards was the hard part. We secretly fashioned tools from everyday items, turning metal scraps into makeshift lock picks. We meticulously worked on the cell door's lock over several weeks and used our limited contact with other prisoners to establish a secret communication network within the fort. Messages were conveyed through whispered words and covert hand signals, linking us into a network of hope and defiance. I gathered what little resources I could: a few strips of cloth for makeshift ropes and a plan to slip out under darkness.

One chilly evening, as we were preparing our escape, a guard caught me in the act. I had just finished tying together a bundle of rags when he appeared, his lantern casting an eerie light over the small, cramped cell. He didn't need to say anything. The look in his eyes was enough. I was hauled out of my cell, my heart racing with a blend of fear and shame.

The punishment was swift and brutal. I was subjected to a public flogging in the courtyard. Each lash of the whip stung painfully. When the flogging ended, I was tossed into solitary confinement. The small, dark cell offered no comfort, only a damp, cold floor and the constant water drip from the ceiling. Each day blended into the next. I lay on the cold stone floor, my body aching and my spirit sinking lower. The isolation was more punishing than the physical pain.

Then, one day, I was abruptly pulled from my cell and told I was being transferred. My heart sank further as I was escorted away from Fort Chambly, only to be transported to what would become my new prison, Prison Island, near Coteau-du-Lac.

Coteau-du-Lac is about forty miles southwest of Montreal on the St. Lawrence River. In those days, it was not a town nor a place of permanence beyond what necessity required. It existed as a rugged outpost, a gathering of soldiers, engineers, and laborers bound together by the work of war. Because of the dangerous rapids, the British built a canal to improve troop and supply movement along the river.

The landscape was dominated by the rhythm of military activity, the clatter of tools shaping the canal and fortifications, and the ceaseless flow of supplies and men. It was a place defined not by homes or families but by function, a transient community built for purpose rather than settlement. Only later, in the quieter decades that followed, would it transform into something enduring, its strategic position drawing settlers to the land shaped by conflict.

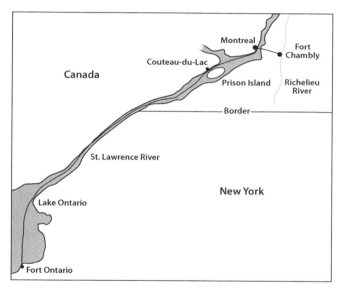

Figure 10 - Captured: Abijah's Route to Fort Chambly and Prison Island

I arrived on the island in the depths of winter, dragged from the relative confines of Fort Chambly with others deemed troublesome enough to warrant removal. The journey was challenging, the cold seeping into our bones long before we reached the icy grip of the St. Lawrence. The sight of the rapids was ominous, their frothing waters framed by the bleak expanse of snow and ice. When the boat carrying us lurched onto the shore, there was no welcome, just the stark reality of where we had been cast.

The first thing I noticed was the blockhouse, an imposing octagonal structure standing in stark contrast to the island's desolation. Built for the British soldiers stationed here, its thick timber walls, steeply sloped roof, and central chimney spoke of a place designed for defense and relative comfort. Within its confines, the soldiers found shelter from the relentless cold, their fire-warmed quarters a far cry from what awaited us prisoners.

The second thing that caught my eye was the stockade, a crude wooden enclosure that penned us in like livestock. Its high, jagged posts formed a stark boundary, offering no shelter or reprieve from the elements. The stockade made it clear that while the soldiers could retreat to the blockhouse, with its warmth and security, we prisoners were left to face the brutal conditions exposed and unprotected. The contrast between these structures was a stark reminder of the divide between captor and captive.

The island itself offered nothing but its harshness. For us, confined within the stockade with no barracks or proper shelters, there was nothing to guard against the biting winds that swept unchallenged across the river. We could only imagine the relative warmth and security inside the blockhouse while we fashioned lean-tos from fallen branches and packed snow for walls. These crude shelters offered scant protection. The snow insulated us as best it could but pressed in on us, a constant reminder of our confinement. Each glance at the blockhouse reinforced the divide between captor and captive, its sturdy walls a bastion for the British and a symbol of the misery we endured in its shadow.

Our fires were meager and stubbornly difficult to maintain. Firewood was scarce, and what little we could gather was often wet and refused to catch. We huddled close to those small flames, sharing what heat they offered. The smoke clung to us, mingling with the stench of unwashed bodies and rotting rations. It was the only warmth we knew, and we clung to it as desperately as we hoped spring would come.

Provisions were meager, consisting of salted pork and hard biscuits that crumbled to dust. When our stomachs gnawed, we scoured the island for anything edible, digging beneath the snow for roots or trapping whatever small creatures might stray too close. Even the bitterest morsel seemed a feast.

Clothing was thin and threadbare, hardly fit for the unrelenting cold. We stuffed the gaps with grass or moss when we could find it, but frostbite claimed several lives nonetheless. Some of us tried to share what blankets and coats we had, though we all suffered the same.

Disease spread quickly in our cramped quarters. Dysentery and fevers took as many as the cold itself, perhaps more. Those who grew too weak faded away, their bodies buried in shallow graves beneath the snow. We marked their passing with quiet solemnity, knowing that any of us might follow.

The isolation was its own torment. The island was silent except for the howling wind and the groan of the ice as it shifted in the river. It became a prison not just of the body but of the mind, where each man was left alone with his fears and regrets. The days bled into one another, marked only by the slow dwindling of our strength.

We survived, those of us who did, not through any abundance of skill or preparation but through sheer will to see another day. The island demanded everything of us, and we gave what we had, though many left more than they could spare. To this day, I do not know how I endured those winters; I only remember that I did, and the memory of that place still chills me more than any frost ever could.

10

Freedom

$\mathcal{A}$s the winds of November 1782 began to chill the shores of Prison Island, we, the captives, could sense that a long-awaited change was in the air. The British, those stern overseers of our confinement, were abuzz with preparations for a meaningful event: the exchange of prisoners.

It all began with negotiations, as it often did. Our representatives, along with those of the British, convened to discuss the terms of the exchange. There were whispers of hope among the captives, for we knew this was our lifeline to freedom.

The terms were decided upon through careful negotiation between the two parties. It was agreed that the exchange would be equal, with prisoners of similar ranks and numbers on both sides. A designated exchange point, a place of safe passage where identities would be verified, was set.

On that day, as the sun rose over the St. Lawrence Seaway, I was led to the waiting boat with my
shackles clinking. The river that had been my captor
for so long was now my route to liberty. The seaway
voyage to Halifax was a trial, but the knowledge that
we were moving closer to freedom filled us with relief
and hope.

And then the news reached me, shared by others
in Halifax. Among the newly mingled prisoners and
fellow passengers, I learned that the war had ended
and victory belonged to the patriots. The surprise was
so profound that it was initially met with disbelief.
But as we were assured that the news was accurate,
it was a joyous revelation that filled our hearts with
hope and the promise of a better tomorrow. Suddenly,
all my trials seemed worth it. We had lost many battles but ultimately won the war.

The ship sailed slowly into Boston Harbor, the
city's skyline stretching before me, familiar but somehow changed. After over two years in prison, I took a
deep breath, savoring the crisp salt air and steadying
myself as we prepared to dock. I'd left a different man,
still a colony subject to the British Crown. Now, I have
returned as a free man to a free city in a country finally
all its own. The war was over, but I could already sense
that the Boston that greeted me was not the one I had
known. My heart swelled with pride, knowing that

my sacrifices, and so many others, had contributed to the birth of this new nation. Yet, the changes were so profound that I felt a sense of disorientation mingling with my wonder.

As I stepped onto the dock, my eyes took in the bustling energy of the pier. Market stalls displayed an array of goods, modest but growing as merchants adapted to new trade networks. Each stand was filled with conversations about opportunity and optimism. Gone were the days when this city simmered with fear and uncertainty. Now, the people's pride was as un-mistakable as red, white, and blue banners fluttering from nearly every corner. American flags, an emblem we'd only dreamed of not long ago, now flew proudly where the Union Jack once reigned. It seemed as if every building and post was draped in symbols of in-dependence, each flag a silent declaration of what we had endured and won.

I walked along the docks, marveling at the faces of those around me. Gone was the mistrust I remem-bered, replaced with a unity I'd never witnessed. The spirit of independence was everywhere, and conversa-tions were excited over what this new country could become. Families and friends gathered, celebrating peace and their role in this shared victory. The faces of Continental soldiers and militiamen greeted me, their worn uniforms telling stories of battles they had returned from, heroes in their city. There was an un-mistakable reverence in how people looked at them, contrasting the days when we were wary of any military presence. These men had become symbols of sacrifice and strength, fighting not for some distant king but for the freedom of those gathered here.

Further inland, I passed the government buildings that had once represented British authority. Now, they bustled with American officials, local leaders, magistrates, and heads of the community who were now serving under a government of our own making. I could barely recognize the people I'd once known working under a king's orders, now meeting openly to discuss how we might shape our future as a new nation. Once alive with grazing cattle and strolling families, the Boston Common showed signs of wear from its use as a training ground for our militia. Still, the open expanse symbolized Boston's strength, as did the men who once served their country as militiamen, levy soldiers, Continentals, or sailors.

Walking these streets, I felt pride and wonder, like seeing Boston for the first time. The people, the spirit, even the air seemed to have changed. Boston had become more than a city. It was now a testament to everything we had fought for, a place of unity, strength, and endless potential. And for the first time, I truly believed this city and this new country were ours.

After my release, my heart brimmed with anticipation for my return to Green River. I was eager to leave the shadow of captivity behind, yearning to return to my simple life as a farmer, to till the land and watch the crops grow.

As I neared the edge of our family farm, I felt my heart pounding against my chest, not from the strain of the long walk home but from a mixture of relief, worry, and longing. It had been nearly three years since I'd left, three years of war, prison, and endless uncertainty. I'd pictured this moment a thousand times, yet now that I was here, the sight of the worn fence and weathered barn felt like a punch to the gut.

The old fence posts sagged, some broken, others mended with whatever branches or scrap wood they could find. I could see where the fields had grown wild along the edges, patches of weeds creeping into the tilled soil. Once solid and proud, our barn looked patched and rough, with mismatched boards on the roof, probably salvaged from an old shed or a neighbor's scrap pile. Still, despite the wear, the place stood, held together by sheer will.

Walking down the familiar path toward the farmhouse, I felt a weight of memories as each step carried me closer to the family I had left behind nearly three years ago. My father had passed in 1777, just after I'd gone to join the fight, and I wondered how that loss had shaped my family in my absence. He had been our cornerstone, a constant presence who toiled alongside us on the land each day, and his loss had created a void I knew my mother and brothers would find hard to fill.

The farmhouse, worn and patched but sturdy, came into view, a homage to the hard work of everyone who'd stayed behind. I noticed right away how much things had changed. Asa had married Elizabeth Graves recently. The family dynamic had shifted with James, our eldest brother, already married to Rhoda. Asa and James, who had taken on much of the fieldwork after our father's death, balanced their work with family responsibilities while still supporting our mother and keeping the farm going.

Bethia and her husband had moved into the farmhouse and taken over its care. My mother remarried in 1780. She married Elijah Hatch, a good man and neighbor, and was raising his children along with my little brother Jacob. Elijah's wife had died the year before during childbirth.

A familiar warmth greeted me inside the house, though the faces were different. My sisters had grown and changed in ways I couldn't have imagined. Bethia had been firmly settled with her husband since 1771. Mary had married John Smith while I was imprisoned, and Hulda, who had been just a girl when I left, was now married to Thomas Paine. They had both become women with homes of their own.

As we sat around the table, each sibling filled me in on what I'd missed, and I realized how the war had reshaped all of us. Our father's death had left my mother at the helm, her strength holding us together. My brothers had stepped into leadership roles on the farm, keeping the land productive and protecting it as best they could while balancing militia duties and their young families. One by one, my sisters had left to marry and start their own lives but hadn't forgotten their roots, often returning to lend a hand.

This wasn't the family I had left. It was something more substantial, something bound by shared struggle and loss. I felt a deep pride swell within me as I looked around, knowing that our family had faced every challenge head-on. We grew in ways we hadn't expected, shaped by hardship and love. I knew I was home, and we could weather whatever came next together.

But another unexpected chapter in my story awaited me when I returned. One sunny Sunday morning, when attending the local church, I could not have anticipated the auspicious encounter ahead as I walked through those hallowed doors. Sitting in one of the pews was a beautiful young lady named Zipporah. Her eyes sparkled like the morning dew, and her smile exuded the gentle warmth of a summer's day. We started a conversation, and it was not long before our hearts became entwined in a tale of love and devotion.

Days turned into weeks and weeks into months. Zipporah and I shared our dreams, our hopes, and our fears. Love blossomed between us, vibrant and undeniable, like spring flowers. It was a love that promised a future filled with the warmth of family, the comfort of home, and the glow of the hearth.

In the fullness of time, Zipporah and I stood in her father's home, pledging our love and commitment to one another. We were wed, two souls brought together by fate and faith, and our journey as husband and wife began.

But, my dear friends, the fullness of this tale is a story for another time. I leave you with this moment when a former prisoner of war, a humble farmer at heart, found his freedom and the love that would shape the rest of his days.

Author's Note

Abijah Virgil's story is the story of the strength, resilience, and unwavering commitment of those who served in the American Revolutionary War. It is etched in the annals of history and has inspired generations.

Abijah's earthly journey ended on November 22, 1837, in Groton, New York. He found his final resting place on a serene knoll in the Luther family burial plot. Today, the plot is located within the Stonehedges Golf Course. His original tombstone, worn over time, was a lasting tribute to his unwavering dedication to his country. The epitaph upon it declared:

IN EARLY LIFE MY COUNTRY CALLED AND ITS VOICE OBEYED, BY FOES MY BODY WAS ENTHRALLED AND NOW IN EARTH IS LAID.

In 2019, the author journeyed to the site only to discover that time had taken its toll on Abijah's tombstone. The tombstone had fractured into three pieces, with the top section pushed into the ground. Acknowledging the importance of preserving his memory, the author contacted the Department of Veterans Affairs for assistance, and a new tombstone was commissioned and installed in 2020, ensuring that Abijah's legacy would endure.

The story of Abijah Virgil and his sacrifices for his country highlights the fortitude and courage of those who built the nation during its early days. Their legacy lives on, etched in stone and engraved in the collective memory of those who honor their sacrifices.

**Figure 11 - Abijah's Headstone,
Stonehedges Golf Course, Groton, New York**

Made in the USA
Las Vegas, NV
08 April 2025

20522012R00090